A FAR DISTANT LAND

The Australian Saga Series
Book One

David Field

SAPERE
BOOKS

A FAR DISTANT LAND

Published by Sapere Books.

20 Windermere Drive, Leeds, England, LS17 7UZ,
United Kingdom

saperebooks.com

ISBN: 978-1-80055-231-9

1

Botany Bay, 1788

Second Lieutenant Daniel Bradbury, New South Wales Marine Corps, leaned back against the starboard gunwales of the *Lady Penrhyn*, eyes front, trying to ignore the chaos all around him. The women were on deck for a brief period of fresh air, prescribed by ship's surgeon Arthur Smyth and they were celebrating their temporary release from the convict hold by dancing and singing bawdy songs. The older ones — or those who were visibly pregnant with children they had not been expecting when they set sail from Portsmouth eight months previously — rested where they could on the decks that heaved gently on the southerly swell that was driving the incoming tide into the bay in which the ship lay at anchor.

Daniel looked across the deck, through the moving throng of women in their shapeless convict sacks, to the port side, where Private McEnery stood leering. Strictly speaking, First Lieutenant Johnston, the only other officer assigned to the vessel, should have been standing in his place, but Daniel felt sure that if he were to count the women on deck, as standing orders decreed that they must, every hour, he would find at least one of them unaccounted for. She would no doubt be below decks with Lieutenant Johnston, and Daniel should by rights report him. Dereliction of duty and fornicating with a prisoner were both serious offences, but George Johnston was senior to him and, besides, Daniel had seen what they did to marines by way of punishment. He had no wish to be the means by which a fellow officer was flogged to the point of near extinction, his back laid bare to the spine by the evil 'cat' whose thongs ended in lead tips.

Daniel looked to his left, over the stern of the vessel, at the land on which they had not yet set foot, for good reason. Down to the very shoreline was a thick mass of tangled vegetation. Beyond the vegetation, in the shallows, were sharp rocks and at low tide it was obvious that this same rock formation jutted out well into the broad bay in which they were anchored. Their fleet commander, Captain Phillip, had been rowed north two days previously — only the day after the *Lady Penrhyn* had limped in behind the rest of the fleet — in search of a better anchorage. He was expected back at any time, since he had taken with him only three small rowing boats and a handful of marines.

Daniel spotted movement in the thick undergrowth a few yards back from the shoreline, as two brown-skinned, near-naked men slid further back into the vegetation, carrying what looked like long spears. The natives were clearly aware of the arrival of the eleven vessels now lying at anchor and they looked far from friendly. Captain Phillip had issued orders that they were not to be harmed in any way unless they offered physical resistance to any landing and Daniel was hoping that he would not have occasion to take the life of any of them.

He was forced to look back inboard when an angry fight broke out among a section of the women. There were at least ten of them involved, so far as he could make out, and he waved an instruction across the deck for Private McEnery to join him in defusing the fray. Two more privates appeared through the hatch that led to the companionway, alerted by the noise, and together they began pulling women from the struggling pile at the foot of the main mast.

Daniel drew his sword and shouted for everyone to remain where they were.

'The rotten cow stole my comb!' a large woman protested.

'That's right — she bin stealin' food an' stuff ever since we come on board!' complained another.

Daniel looked down at the object of these accusations — the woman who had been at the bottom of the pile. She was no more than twenty-five years old, insofar as it was possible to tell beneath the grime of eight months that covered her face. There was blood running down to her chin from several nail gouges on her cheeks. 'Get up,' Daniel ordered.

The girl shook her head in defiance and bits of sawdust and straw flew out of her long black locks. 'I ain't been stealing, as God and the Holy Mother are my witnesses!' she protested.

'We can arrange witnesses closer to hand than that,' Daniel replied. He looked down towards the stern, where his eyes came to rest on two older women who had been watching quietly, seated on coiled ropes. 'You two!' he called out to them. 'Take this young woman to the foc'sle and search her for the comb she's accused of stealing, then bring her back here.'

Two minutes later, they returned, the greyer of the two women shaking her head.

'She ain't got no comb, sir,' the woman told him.

The girl smiled up at him with near perfect teeth. 'Now didn't I just say that?'

'She's a lying cunny!' one of her original accusers screamed and the women around her began yelling their agreement.

'Silence!' Daniel ordered, his hand on his sword hilt. He turned to the three privates who had been a silent audience to what had been transpiring. 'Take all the women below — except this one. I have further questions of her.'

Amid curses and yells of protest, the rest of the women were bundled down the companionway and secured below decks in their wooden caged 'messes'.

Daniel instructed the young woman to accompany him to the stern and invited her to sit on one of the rope coils. He looked down at her with a stern expression. 'Name?'

'Mary Murphy — sir.'

'And *were* you stealing?'

The girl rolled her eyes in supplication as she replied, 'Haven't I already sworn before God and the Holy Mother that I'm innocent? And me a good Catholic girl that was brought up never to take the holy names in vain.'

'You sound Irish,' Daniel said, a little nonplussed to find such a pious young girl among a boatload of foul-mouthed, violent women.

'That's because I am,' Mary replied with a twinkling smile. 'All the way from County Fermanagh, where me mother — God rest her blessed soul — was a washerwoman to the Bishop.'

'Why would all those women falsely accuse you of stealing?' Daniel asked, intrigued.

'Because I'm not like them,' Mary replied. 'I don't swear, I won't lie with the guards for extra rations, and I say me prayers every night before I lay down to sleep.'

'Do they bully you, like they were doing just now?'

'All the time, sir. They steal me food, they pull me hair and — worst of all — they mock me prayers.'

'How did a sweet thing like you come to be on a convict ship?'

Mary looked down. 'No one's called me a sweet thing since me long-dead intended died in the potato famine that drove me to London to seek me living as a nursemaid. I had two little sisters as well, you see, and I was fully wise to how to bring up weans. And that's how I came to be here, in a manner of speaking. But you'll not be interested in a tale of a poor innocent girl done wrong, will ye now?'

'Go on,' Daniel invited her.

'Well, like I said, I was working as a nursemaid to this charming family in Chelsea. They had a lovely little boy — Jamie his name was — and it was like he was my own. Anyway, the master of the house, he wanted more from me than looking after his only child. One evening while the lady of the house was away visiting, he tried his luck with me, if you know what I mean. I told him no and thought that would be the end of it, but he hid one of his wife's best jewels under the bed in me room, and then called in the constables to search the house. I was taken up, and the jury didn't believe me, but the old judge took pity on me — and here I am.'

'That's terrible,' Daniel said, nodding in sympathy, 'and I'm willing to bet you're not the only one on board this vessel who's been the victim of that sort of injustice. I can only express my concern at your misfortune, but I can't make the law go backwards.'

'At the end of the day,' Mary said, 'it may be for the best. I'd have spent me life just as a servant to some fancy household or other, but out here in this new land — well, who knows? I might find a husband or something, or at least a strong man to protect me and give me little ones. The worst thing is that I'll never see poor Jamie again — it was like he was me own, and he cried when they took me away with me hands tied in front of me.'

Just then there came the sound of cannon fire from the *Supply*, which Captain Phillip had converted into his flagship a week out from landing because it had proved to be the fastest vessel in the fleet. Other vessels fired answering shots and the master of the *Lady Penrhyn*, William Sever, interrupted their conversation with important news: 'The Captain's returning. Please God we can at long last tread dry land.'

Daniel escorted Mary to the companionway hatch and ordered one of the convict guards to take her back down to her mess.

'Perhaps you should remain down there for a while, to prevent her being misused by those who falsely accuse her,' Daniel instructed him.

Mary reached out a warm soft hand and touched his left cheek as she walked past him. 'God bless you, kind soul,' she murmured as she flashed him a beautiful smile through white teeth, her green eyes wide with gratitude.

Daniel flushed and looked down at the deck.

Early the next morning, the order came to raise anchor and follow the *Supply* north. The hatches were kept down as they battered their way into the southerly swell once they had left the relatively calm bay and rolled their way north. After only a few minutes a wide opening appeared on their port beam, with imposing wooded headlands on either side. The vessels ahead of them steered to port and headed in between the headlands, the *Lady Penrhyn* following behind, almost the last in the queue of ships. Within minutes of passing between the headlands, the wind had eased, and the swell had dropped sufficiently for the men on deck to release their holds on the gunwales as they took in the long wide estuary that their commander had chosen in preference to the forbidding rocks of Botany.

Ahead of them, the *Supply* had already dropped anchor and her boats had been lowered to enable an advance party to stride up the beach. As Daniel strained to look forward across the mile or so of water, listening absentmindedly to the now familiar rattle of their own anchor chain being played out, he saw a tall pine tree fall into the stunted scrub that lay just beyond the beach. Men with axes immediately set about trimming it, while others could be seen putting some of the tools they had brought with them to good use, digging a deep hole in the sand.

An hour later, Daniel caught the distant strain of a bugler blowing his lungs out in a patriotic celebration, as the Union Jack fluttered out at the top of the recently erected flagpole, to the accompaniment of a volley of celebratory musket shots.

Later, all the marine officers were ordered on board the *Sirius* for a meeting with their commanding officer, Major Ross. There was insufficient room below decks, so the men stood, sat, or simply squatted on their haunches, as Major Ross squinted his eyes against the glaring sun and began by advising them that now they had finally made landfall, his role had changed, along with the role to be played by all his men.

'We are now a land-based penal colony,' he told them, 'and His Majesty has graciously appointed me lieutenant-governor of the colony, directly under Captain Phillip as the governor. But my day-to-day responsibilities will still include the command of the Marine Corps and we are met here today in order that I may instruct you on what you will be required to do once we are on shore.'

'Are we mooring here for good, sir?'

'Please God that we are,' Ross replied. 'I'm sure that we're all looking forward to feeling firm ground beneath our boots once more, even though we *are* marines. And Governor Phillip, as he is now to be addressed, has deemed this to be the ideal anchorage. As you will already have realised, this is a safe and copious natural harbour, with a generous beach for landing and unloading, a ready supply of fresh water from a stream that flows into the bay and soil that appears to hold out some prospect of yielding crops. The water that we are currently treading he has named "Sydney Cove" and the settlement we are to build on land has already been named "Port Jackson".

'But a colony will not appear either naturally, or overnight. We need to establish houses for shelter, roads for transport and crops for grazing and eating. The supplies we brought with us should last until fresh crops are harvested and we have tools with which to dig the ground, quarry rock, fell trees and build houses. The labour for all this will come from the male convicts, who will be organised into working parties, which *you* must guard, not only from any prospect of escape by the convicts, but also against the natives who have been glaring out of the undergrowth at us ever since we arrived. There is to be no shooting at them unless we are under attack, but something tells me that such a day is not far distant.'

'What about the female convicts, sir?' Daniel asked.

'Ah yes, the ladies. They will obviously work on tasks for which women are best fitted. Washing, cooking, sewing and rearing children.'

'And screwing,' came a quiet voice from one side and a rousing cheer went up.

Major Ross stood with a stern face until it had quietened down. 'I remind you that fraternising with female prisoners is a court-martial offence. It is also likely to lead to disease and unwanted pregnancy. I realise that all the men in this expedition have been without women for a long time but this is a newly established colony under the British Crown, not the Vauxhall Pleasure Gardens. The women may be convicts, but they are still women and entitled to our protection in the normal way of things.

'Anyway, as to the detailed ordering of matters, each of the lieutenants will be placed in charge of an aspect of the many duties that have to be allocated. To begin with, the male convicts will be taken off in work groups, guarded in a ratio of forty prisoners to one marine. Several such groups will fall under the overall command of a lieutenant, to whom will be allocated the ranks beneath them, to be spread between the workgroups as he thinks fit. I have already drawn up and copied the group allocations and these will be handed out to you in due course.

'If you have any questions regarding the way in which these allocations have been made, please ask either myself or Captain Mulgrave. We will meet every day under the flag, in order to discuss progress; the signal for the meeting will be three cannon shots from the *Sirius*. Very well, dismiss, men and welcome to Port Jackson.'

Daniel was relieved to discover that his command included ongoing supervision of the female convicts on board the *Lady Penrhyn*. It was not the only vessel that contained female convicts, but it held the bulk of them, and at least it was not being abandoned to the lecherous attentions of some of the lieutenants.

Daniel put his two best privates on daily guard duties, assisted by ship's crew members who now had nothing else to do and were more than content to amuse themselves down in the convict holds, where they could expose themselves to venereal disease, cholera, lice and verbal abuse. Daniel's orders were that the women be brought up twice daily, after meals, to exercise — and if possible, wash — if the weather was fine and not so hot as to be hazardous to health. With that, he ordered a ship's boat to be lowered and made his first journey ashore.

He was met on the beach by the major's adjutant, who had seen him being rowed ashore and who handed him several lists of convicts and the marines allocated to guard them. They had been consigned to hut building, rock quarrying and tree felling, and there were three groups in all, totalling one hundred and twenty men.

Daniel instructed his marine privates to round up all the men as they came off the ships' cutters bobbing out in the bay and then climbed onto the tailboard of one of the ox carts that had been unloaded from the supply ship *Fishburn* the previous day. Once they all appeared to be standing below him, in knotted, sullen, ill-clad clusters, he raised his voice to be heard. 'You have all been allocated to tasks with which most of you will be unfamiliar. Be assured that I will not punish inability. I *will*, however, punish laziness, insubordination and deliberate obstruction. Plus, of course, any attempt at escape will result in death, either from a musket ball in the back, or on the gallows that I have no doubt will be the first thing to be constructed here on land.

'I have a list of all you men who will be working under my command, with an armed marine to enforce my instructions. Some of you list your previous occupations, some of you not. Let's begin with the obvious first step. Raise your hand if you are a tree feller.'

Several hands rose in the air and Daniel instructed them to stand in a separate group to one side.

'Now, any quarry workers or stonemasons?'

Another group was separated from the main body and there was one task left.

'House builders and thatchers?'

This produced the third group and some fifty men now stood aside from the main body of convicts.

Daniel chose the oldest looking man in each of the specialised teams and invited each of them, in turn, to select labourers from among those who were left. Within ten minutes he had three working parties, each headed by a man who claimed to have experience. He then turned to the marines who had been watching the proceedings. 'Private Milward, take the group into the trees over there and start felling. Private Kenning, you've got the quarry working party. Find a suitable outcrop of rock and start them on cutting. Private Webber, you're with me and the house-builders. All of you report to Captain Mulgrave on the shoreline down there and tell him what tools you need to have unloaded from the supply ships.'

Before long, Daniel was distracted by shouting from the forest. He looked up to see Private Milward anxiously beckoning him over. Daniel strode quickly over to where a man lay on the ground, clutching his bare foot, white in the face and breathing rapidly and shallowly.

'Sir, this man has been bitten by some sort of serpent,' Private Milward explained, himself white in the face. 'I saw it myself, slithering into that long grass over there.'

Daniel looked down at the man. 'Show me the wound,' he said.

The man removed his hand from the area of flesh just above his left ankle, which had two holes in it, about half an inch apart and oozing blood. The man sank back onto the earth, shivering uncontrollably and whimpering in fear and self-pity. Daniel stripped off his red dress coat, tore a strip from his shirt sleeve and knelt beside the man. He looked back up at Milward with instructions to watch carefully, then bent his head over the wound. He sucked as much blood as he could from the wound without swallowing it, spat it out onto the ground and repeated the process four times before pausing for breath. He looked back up at Milward. 'Do you think you could do what I just did, three times?'

Milward turned pale again, but nodded and replaced Daniel beside the injured man, while Daniel busied himself twisting his ripped shirt strip into a tight bandage. As Milward's head came up for the third time, Daniel tied the bandage as tightly as he could around the victim's leg, just above the puncture mark. He looked back down at the man's face and asked, 'Does it feel as if you've suddenly lost all feeling in your foot?'

The man nodded and Daniel stood up.

'Good,' he said, 'that means that the circulation has stopped. Hopefully the poison won't spread any further, but this man must be carried down to the shoreline immediately and handed over to the nearest ship's surgeon, preferably one who's served in the tropics, which is where I learned that little trick. In the meantime, tell the men to watch where they put their feet — even the ones with boots or shoes on.'

'Yes, sir,' Milward replied, ashen-faced as he beckoned two men over and detailed them to carry their colleague down to the shore with a request for a surgeon.

When Daniel climbed back up the rope ladder onto the deck of the *Lady Penrhyn*, it was almost dark. He called immediately for the mess allocation chart for the convict deck. Unable to find Mary Murphy's name on it, but well aware of the clerical incompetence of naval personnel assigned to non-naval duties, he climbed down the companionway, gritting his teeth against the stench and walked down the middle gangway between the messes that looked for all the world like animal pens at a country market. Each mess contained ten women and was constructed out of thick wooden staves that ran from the floor of the convict deck to the roof, which was of course the floor of the main deck above it. The staves were like a fence through which one could keep an eye on the mess from the outside, but each mess had a heavy metal lock set into its solid entrance door.

As he walked down the centre aisle, he was subjected to the same verbal insults, lewd catcalls and carefully aimed spits that all his men had to endure and to which even he had become inured over the months. Halfway down on the left, he saw Mary sitting crouched in the far corner of her mess, with the rest of the women who were locked in with her gossiping among themselves. They looked up as he stopped by the entrance door, turned back to the guard with him who was carrying the keys and lantern and ordered him to unlock the mess door without opening it. While this was being done, he pointed sternly at Mary and shouted an order, 'You! Out!'

Looking scared, Mary scrambled to her feet and scuttled to the door. Daniel nodded and the door was opened for long enough to enable Mary to squeeze out before it was slammed shut behind her. Daniel took her arm and guided her back towards the companionway.

Back up on deck, Daniel released her arm and smiled down at her. 'Forgive my ungracious manner down there, but I didn't want them to think that you were being singled out for special treatment, or they'd only have made your life a further misery. Are the other women in Mess 11 the only ones who bully you?'

'Yes — why?'

'Can you cook? Tomorrow morning I have to send forty women ashore to work in the mess tent, preparing food for the men on the work details. If I send you as one of the forty and

17

leave the rest of those dreadful women in Mess 11 where they are, you'd be free of their persecution, wouldn't you?'

She stared at him for a moment as she took in the full import of what he was telling her, then tears began to well in her eyes and one rolled down her cheek as she nodded.

'God bless you, sir. What's your name, so that I can pray to God to bring down eternal blessings upon you for your kindness?'

'Daniel — it's Daniel.'

'Well, Daniel, if there's anything a poor lass like me can ever do for you, just say the word.'

'You might not think that, when you're out there in the heat, working over open fires and suchlike,' Daniel replied. 'As for tonight, I don't think it would be a good idea for you to go back below decks. If you stay above decks tonight, we can just slip you in with the others detailed for the onshore cooking tent when we bring them on deck at first light.'

He looked around the ship's deck and his eyes rested on a ship's cutter hanging from a pulley and lashed down to the inside of the port gunwales. He walked over to it and lifted the canvas that kept the rain out of its scuppers. He turned back towards Mary and pointed down inside it.

'You can sleep under there. I'll go and get you my cloak, to wrap yourself in when the night air turns colder, just before dawn. As soon as the sky lightens in the morning, slide out from under and go and stand near the companionway hatch, as if you'd just been ordered up on deck.'

Mary reached out to him. 'Couldn't you get under there with me and keep me safe?'

Daniel looked carefully up and down the main deck. It was deserted. He allowed Mary to guide him by the hand and they both crawled under the canvas, where Mary immediately rolled into his arms. Daniel felt a warm glow of contentment as he held her to him and finally fell asleep with the musky smell of her long black hair in his nostrils.

The next morning they woke at the same time and slid out from under the canvas onto the main deck. Mary scuttled to the foc'sle and Daniel went below decks to the Lieutenant's cabin in order to shave and change into his spare shirt. When he came back on deck, George Johnston was standing under the main mast with a dark-haired young woman with a long, handsome, but serious face. She was carrying a small child and looking nervous.

'This is Esther,' Johnston told Daniel. 'I hope you don't mind, but I've added her to your list to go ashore on the cooking detail. The convict hold is hardly a healthy place for her young daughter — or anyone else, for that matter. I see you've already selected one for yourself from down there.' He gestured to where Mary was huddling under the foremast, trying to look inconspicuous.

Daniel waved her over. 'Stand here, next to Esther,' he instructed her. 'The rest'll come up after two bells, but I'm afraid you two ladies will have to forego your usual sumptuous breakfast.'

Forty minutes later, as the last of the line of embarkees was being assisted down the rope ladder into the third boat of the morning to cast off for the shore, Mary and Esther were the final two in the line. They halted briefly, each awaiting the hand of a seaman to assist them over the side and Mary reached up quickly, pulled Daniel's head down by the collar of his tunic and kissed him on the cheek.

'Thank you for selecting me, Daniel,' she whispered. 'I'll make sure you don't regret it.'

2

Daniel stood silently to attention at the head of his column, the four lines abreast that had been ordered out onto the new parade ground in front of the temporary marine barracks on the north bank of the Cove. In reality, the 'barracks' consisted merely of a row of tents pitched among the rocks, but at least those rocks gave them partial protection against the gales that swept in from the north. However, on days like today, when the wind was from the south-east, the canvas flapped angrily in the gale and the peg lines threatened to pull free completely from the loose sand into which they had been hammered. Periodically a tent would blow down in weather such as this, which did nothing for the image of the regiment as an efficient fighting force.

The drum began to beat slowly, as Private Fraser was stripped of his uniform jacket and blindfolded. Then, escorted by two fellow privates, he was marched slowly up and down between the ranks to the remorseless beat of the drum. This was his penalty for being caught in a female tent only yards from the barracks, but closer to the rocky shoreline. He was being 'drummed out' of the regiment and would now have to fend for himself, entitled to neither military fare nor convict rations. He was lucky that he was not being either flogged or hanged.

The men were dismissed and Daniel wandered back towards the shoreline, past where a team of convicts, under instruction from a ship's carpenter, was erecting the prefabricated frame for the governor's house which had been brought from Portsmouth on the *Borrowdale* and only required further timber from the forest behind in order to be complete, after which his furniture could be installed. It would be the first complete construction in the colony, but would be followed eventually by a stone replacement for which foundations were already being dug on the south side and in front of which a garden plot was already marked out. Lesser mortals would be allocated to the many huts that were under construction further back up the beach.

It was approaching the middle of the day and there was already a bustle of activity in and around the mess tent, inside which Daniel knew he would find Mary, but the handful of men detailed to transport the prepared food to the work parties were not under his direct command and he had no excuse to be wandering over there.

He stopped briefly amid all the hustle and bustle around him and asked himself why he was even contemplating seeking out a single convict woman, when he had been responsible for over a hundred of them while they had been at sea. He could pretend to himself, if he chose, that he was merely ensuring that those who had persecuted her had not been allocated to the mess tent, and to a certain degree that was the case. They were into their third week ashore and all the remaining women were now on land, allocated to washing the clothes of the convict labourers and sewing up the tears in their rudimentary garments caused by the rough work that they were carrying out.

Some of the women had small children, like the one who George Johnston had obviously taken a fancy to, and a separate tent had been allocated to nursing mothers and pregnant women, to whom had been allocated lighter duties. There were some one hundred and fifty women ashore and rumour had it that the vessels that had brought them here would soon be raising anchor and sailing out of the cove, so why was he constantly thinking back in his mind to the time they had all spent on board? If he was to be brutally honest with himself, he couldn't completely erase from his mind the memory of that cool night under the canvas, in which he had held in his arms one of the most strikingly beautiful women he had ever laid eyes on.

He found himself just outside the mess tent, looking through its flap in a subconscious search for Mary. Inside was all steam and bustle, as men came and went with pots of stew and loaves of freshly-baked bread whose wafting aroma made Daniel's stomach rumble. There was a hiss from somewhere and he located the source of the sound at the far side of the mess tent; Mary was waving to him and beckoning him over to where she stood, almost completely hidden by the side canvas. He walked over to speak to her and as he got closer he could see the sweat running down her face in rivulets from under the coarse bonnet into which her luxuriant black hair had been crammed. There were sweat stains under the armpits of the simple brown gown that she had somehow acquired to replace the rice sacks in which she had been clad when he last saw her, but she seemed so pleased to see him that she didn't care about her appearance.

She grinned at him and brought her other hand from behind her back to reveal within it a sizeable bread bun. 'Good day, guardian angel. I hope you like cheese, for this one has half a block baked into it. I made it just for you.'

'Thank you, Mary,' Daniel murmured as he took the loaf from her and began eating hungrily. It was the best thing he'd consumed since their embarkation dinner at The Partridge on Portsmouth dockside. He swallowed the portion he had chewed off, cleared his mouth and asked, 'Are they treating you properly in there?'

'Yes, thanks to you. The work's hot and hard, but the days pass quickly enough.' Mary looked him up and down appraisingly. 'You're thinner than when I last saw you.'

Daniel realised that he might be getting her into trouble, standing there openly eating a loaf of bread that she'd obviously purloined from the mess tent and keeping her from her duties. He was about to thank her again politely and walk away when she asked: 'So how come I see you every day, walking up that hill? Have you got a woman hidden up there in the trees?'

Daniel blushed. 'No woman — just eighty or so convicts felling trees and building huts.'

'Who'll be living in them?'

'No idea — officers and marines, I suppose.'

'And will you get one all to yourself, so you can hold lassies tight against the night air?'

'I really have no idea,' Daniel replied, then realised that he'd left half the question unanswered and that clarification was needed. 'What I mean is, I don't know how many men will be allocated to huts. As for women, there are strict rules against cohabitation — I just watched a marine drummed out of the regiment for doing just that.'

Half an hour later, Daniel was watching the men on the building detail, under the half-hearted supervision of Private Webber, who'd been excused attendance at the drumming out parade. One hut was virtually complete, with the final few slabs being nailed into place by a couple of sweaty convicts whose previously fair skin had turned a bright lobster red as the result of three weeks of labouring under the remorseless sun. The rain didn't seem to come until late in the afternoon and was usually accompanied by thunder and lightning, so it had been possible to move ahead with the hut construction almost without delay, hampered only by the periodic shortage of materials from the forest behind them, in which the occasional curious tanned face could be seen peering out from the vegetation, looking for a chance to steal a valuable tool. Several other huts were in various stages of completion and things were obviously going well.

'How soon d'you reckon that one'll be finished?' came a voice from behind him.

Daniel turned round and there stood George Johnston with a big self-satisfied grin on his boyish face.

'By the end of the day, probably,' Daniel told him. 'Why do you want to know?'

George looked longingly past him at the nearly completed hut and replied without averting his gaze. 'When it's completed, get one of the men to carve a nameplate above the door that reads "First Lieutenant George Johnston, Adjutant to the Governor".'

'I thought Major Ross already had an adjutant.'

'He does, but the governor wanted one of his own and I got selected. Mainly because the governor and Ross can't even agree on what day it is. If it were left to Ross, we'd be building a massive stockade against the natives and taking pot shots every time they appeared. Seems that Governor Phillip can't even be civil in Ross's presence and he needed someone to relay his instructions, so I became his message boy. In return, I get the first hut that's available, to denote my exalted rank and emphasise the importance of the office of the governor himself. I'm now supervising the erection of that fine stone house he's going to be living in.'

'Congratulations,' Daniel replied woodenly, concerned to learn of the conflict between the two most important men in the colony.

'Anyway, Esther and I can move in tomorrow, by the sound of things.' George looked back at Daniel for the first time. 'Esther's expecting again — mine, this time,' he announced proudly, 'and I've been allowed to select a goat from the herd grazing in the garden where the governor's stone mansion's going to be. That'll supply her first-born, Roseanna, with milk, but she's going to need a nursemaid while Esther deals with the new arrival. Any ideas? You saw more of the women below decks than I did.'

Daniel was about to point out that George had obviously seen more of one particular woman than anyone had, but checked himself when he thought back to his recent conversation with Mary. 'There's that one you saw me with on deck just before we took the first party ashore — "Mary", her name is and she was telling me how much she misses acting as a substitute mother for her two young sisters. She seems pretty well domesticated.'

George gave him a knowing leer. 'I *thought* I saw you chatting to her outside the mess tent when I was looking over there a while ago. Can't blame you for favouring a bonnie one like that — when we move into this hut, which hopefully will be tomorrow, send her over to meet Esther. If she's any good and doesn't list infant murder among her convictions, she may be just the ticket.'

'We aren't — that is, we're not...' Daniel started to explain, before George silenced him with a wave of his hand.

'Don't bother trying to explain, Daniel — just send the lassie over to see Esther tomorrow.'

Daniel gave instructions that the first hut was to be completed that evening, with an internal wall that would create two rooms, then walked back to the mess tent. He stood at the front flap and waited until Mary caught his eye as she bent over the large pot she was scrubbing out. She walked out of the tent wiping her hands on an apron cloth.

'If you've come for my dumplings, I have to disappoint you. We just put the baking fire out, so you'll just have to go hungry until tomorrow.'

'It's not that,' Daniel explained. 'Not that I don't fancy your dumplings,' he added hastily, inwardly cursing his clumsiness with words whenever he was talking with Mary. As Mary grinned back at him, he explained all about George, Esther, the existing daughter and the baby she was expecting. 'This is a real opportunity for you to better yourself in this dreadful place and if you discharge your duties well, who knows where you could finish up?'

'Married to an officer meself, you mean?' Mary asked under lowered eyelids.

'Like I said — who knows?' Daniel blushed. 'I can't do any more for you than I have already, so it'll be up to you how you progress from here.'

Mary's face fell as she took in the import of his words. 'Are you telling me that I'll not be seeing you again?'

For the next week, Daniel deliberately spent more time at the quarry that had been opened up a mile or so away from the main camp. There was now a need for large building blocks for the governor's mansion on the south side of the cove and the rock strata out at what was called the 'Brick Field' was deep and plentiful. The masons were able to supervise the splitting of long sections vertically off each outcrop by hammering wooden pegs down into it until it split. Then they took their hammers and cold chisels and cut it into heavy sections that were approximately three feet high and two feet thick, which were then carted down the slope to where the new mansion was beginning to rise from its base in the firm rock a few hundred yards back from the high-water mark. The waste rock that came with each cut was also carted away, to be tipped into the sea at the shore's edge in order to make a deep-water wharf at which ocean-going ships could be moored.

Daniel had other reasons to be at the quarry. While he was supervising the work, he was not required to stand in front of the hut into which George and Esther had moved with their daughter, who was now being nursed by Mary. She'd been eagerly employed by Esther and every day Mary could be seen around the outside of the hut, carrying her tiny charge in her arms and walking up and down in the warm sunlight, seemingly content with her new duties. She'd waved Daniel over the first time and cheekily reminded him that he was not getting any younger and should be thinking of having one of his own.

He found himself horribly confused, but strangely excited, by her references to settling down, and her guile in expressing things in such a way as to sound as if she were offering herself to him on a plate. He had only once lost his heart to a young woman and the pain of rejection had hit him so hard that he had taken the King's shilling and found himself on board a navy frigate heading west. Heaven only knew what might happen the next time, and this beautiful young Irish girl was too good to be true. He dared not let their relationship develop, only to find that he was rejected again, with nowhere to run to this time.

Satisfied that the quarrying was proceeding well enough, he walked down the slope and into the forest area to the left, in which there should have been a dozen or so men felling trees. It was curiously inactive, with no customary 'thunk' of axes, no sound of sawing and no cries of warning as pines and other trees came crashing down into the lower foliage. Then he became aware of a chorus of raised voices and saw a group of convicts in a circle a few hundred yards into the trees. He sensed that something was not quite right and quickened his pace, calling out to Private James Milward, who was watching what was going on in bewilderment, but had his bayonet fixed and pointed at something on the ground.

Daniel reached the group and looked down at a native youth, aged probably in his late teens or early twenties. He was leaning up on one elbow, staring fearfully at the end of Milward's bayonet, while several of the convicts appeared to be threatening the man with their axes.

'What's going on?' Daniel demanded.

'This savage, sir,' Milward told him. 'The men caught him trying to steal an axe. I'd have shot him, but we've been ordered to conserve our powder. Do you want him bayoneted?'

'No,' Daniel replied, 'for several reasons. The first is that we can hardly expect these people to behave towards us other than savagely if we behave like savages *ourselves*. The second is that we don't know how many more of his tribe are hiding in the bushes and thickets all around us. We are less than twenty in number and between us we have only two muskets and a handful of axes. Do *you* want to take that risk, Private?'

'No, sir,' Milward replied, as he brought his musket back into the upright position.

The young native's eyes travelled from the tip of the bayonet to Daniel's face, as he awaited his fate, having clearly identified Daniel as the leader. Daniel walked up to him and leaned forward with an outstretched hand. The youth took his hand and Daniel pulled him to his feet.

'Friend,' Daniel said.

The youth smiled, then took off like a startled deer into the forest, leaping through the large bushes as if they didn't exist.

'Consider my debt repaid,' George said to Daniel as he walked towards him outside the quarry the following morning.

'What do you mean?' Daniel asked as he wiped the sweat from his brow, then replaced his tricorn hat before the sun could burn through to his scalp again.

'Major Ross wants you placed on a charge for your failure to kill a native who was attempting to steal our valuable equipment. Private Milward was forced to tell the whole story when one of the convicts spread the word about your seeming dereliction of duty. Seems that our Major doesn't want to see any of our neighbours left alive and he's quietly raging that you let one go. I told him that you didn't want to provoke a skirmish while we were seriously outnumbered, which is the way Milward told me the story. To cut another long story short, Ross has left the punishment to me, so consider yourself punished.'

'And how did you come to be in my debt anyway?' Daniel asked.

'That new nursemaid you sent us — Martha. She's quite the ticket, according to Esther, who's taken to her like a duck to water. Seems they come from the same part of London, which was of course a bonus, but apparently Martha's already got

Roseanna eating out of her hand — literally — and Esther's very grateful to you. As, indeed, am I.'

'I'm not sure we're talking about the same person,' Daniel replied, confused. 'The girl I sent to you is called Mary and she's from Ireland. Did you finish up hiring someone else?'

George stared at him for a moment, then burst out laughing. 'Is that what she told you? My good man, her name is Martha Mallett and she's from Shoreditch.'

'Are you *sure*?' Daniel demanded, a sinking feeling developing in the pit of his stomach.

'Of course I'm sure. You don't think I'd invite someone to live in our hut without checking out her background? I consulted the convict records in the governor's possession and she's Martha Mallett, a convicted thief, pickpocket and swindler, from Shoreditch, in London.'

'But she *sounds* Irish,' Daniel objected, now far from sure of his ground.

'She was also an actress, according to Esther,' George explained. 'In fact, what makes her so agreeable to Esther is the way she can imitate all sorts of characters at the drop of a hat. She had Esther in positive hysterics by pretending to be the governor's wife — a high-born lady with hoity-toity manners and a runny nose. She also does a nice line in costermonger slang, should you be interested.'

'And she's a thief, you say?' Daniel persevered, his anger mounting by the second.

'A pickpocket,' George elaborated. 'And a swindler. She finally got transported rather than hanged because she amused her trial judge with the story of her last exploit, when she apparently got a bishop to part with his under-drawers. How droll can *that* be?'

Daniel's face set like the sandstone rocks all around them, as he looked round at George. 'May I ask another favour of you, George?'

'Ask away,' George agreed, still chuckling.

'Keep that damned whore out of my sight!' Daniel bellowed, as he stormed off up the quarry entrance.

3

By the end of February, the governor's house had been completed. It was a large building, constructed principally from the prefabricated frame that had come out with the fleet, supplemented with local timber that a ship's carpenter had carefully hewn into floorboards, internal panelling and room dividers. For the governor of an entire colony, it was a modest enough affair, but compared with the simple huts into which marines and convicts had been consigned as fast as they had been constructed, it was a veritable palace.

It would not, in any case, be the final abode of the governor, who was taking a daily interest in the sandstone blocks that were rapidly being placed on top of each other further round the bay, in order to form the second stone-built edifice in the colony, in which he would eventually take up residence. But it was the first house of any size and the governor ordered a general celebration, partly to acknowledge the progress that had been made and partly to lift the morale of the convicts. There was to be music, dancing and feasting, and an entire ox had been slaughtered in order to feed the multitude — or, at least, those who came early enough — while loaf after loaf had been baked in the newly constructed oven in the mess tent. The alcohol was strictly limited to one tot of rum per male and one glass of ale per female, but the natural gaiety of the occasion caused many to behave as if they were drunk.

Daniel had opted to continue living in an officer's tent, refusing all offers of a hut in the same settlement area in which the other officers had taken up residence. He was determined to keep away from any possible contact with Mary — or was it

Martha now? — after the way she had deceived him. He had been drawn into a similar web by his former employer's older daughter, Alice, who had led him on with smiles, winks and knowing looks, while all the time allowing her father to negotiate a more suitable match with a wealthy trade associate. When Daniel had plucked up the courage to declare his love, she had pretended to be honoured and had even contrived to cry, but had firmly advised him that she was to be betrothed to another.

He had been led on again, he realised, and if he was ever to know happiness with a woman, he would have to harden his heart against their simple but effective guiles. Martha had used him to obtain more favourable circumstances and God knew how many other men she had similarly deceived. He had no hope of escaping her delicious web if he allowed himself any further contact with her; his only hope was to avoid her completely and take the first opportunity that presented itself to leave this dreadful place where physical proximity and shared hardship led inevitably to ill-advised liaisons.

It was in a dark humour that Daniel ducked under the flap of the tent that he shared with several other marines and stepped out onto the area of beach where the celebrations were being held, late in the afternoon of what had been a hot and sultry February day. The sky, as he gazed south over the cove, was as black as his mood. The sullen black wall of cloud that was slowly drifting towards him seemed to be gaining strength by the minute, with an occasional lightning flash ripping through it.

There were couples dancing wherever he looked and his ears were tortured by the raucous cacophony of several fiddlers — and an accordion player — each playing for the amusement of a dancing group. But each of them was playing a different tune, in a different key, at a different time, and from a distance the overall effect was like being in a madhouse, with demented demons shrieking out a tuneless dirge to please their Satanic master.

Daniel skirted round a couple who were writhing and grunting in the sand and further down the beach Daniel could clearly make out the distant figures of George and Esther, with Martha standing alongside nursing their daughter. Esther was seated on a rock, fanning herself against the strength-sapping humidity, while George stood chatting to Major Ross. A few feet away was the governor himself, proudly surveying the proceedings and nodding condescendingly at the antics of his prisoners. Daniel sneered at their pomposity and allowed himself one more glance towards Martha.

She looked up at that moment and jerked her head in a gesture of invitation for him to join their group, but he looked away. Daniel wanted nothing to do with any of them. He stalked off down the beach, stepping round groups of revellers and clusters of helplessly drunken convicts who had obviously contrived some way of obtaining extra grog.

The storm was only minutes away, he noted, as he looked up at the sky. The black had turned to a dark grey and in the far distance, over where they had dropped their first anchor in Botany Bay, the sheets of rain were already lashing the coastline. He finished his food and began to walk back towards his own tent, intent on getting under cover before the storm hit, but just then there was a huge flash, followed almost immediately by a deafening bang. The rain began to descend in one continuous sheet and the gale sweeping across the bay began to lift up the skirts of both convict women and the few ladies in attendance, clearly no respecter of rank or dignity. Instinctively Daniel looked across at where he had seen

George's party in the rocks and saw George take the child from Martha and shepherd the group against the driving rain towards the newly constructed governor's house, where they clearly intended to take shelter.

Martha had hesitated and then begun to run after them. She appeared to stumble over the outstretched legs of an insensible drunk and fell heavily into the sand. A flash of lightning hit the beach only yards from her and sand spun into the air as another massive bang threatened to shatter Daniel's eardrums. He raced across the beach to where Martha lay, her face wreathed in pain, clutching her shoulder. The bonnet she had been wearing earlier had been blown away and her long black hair was drenched by the rain. She caught Daniel's eye as she lay there and the imploring look on her face was more than he could bear.

Running the last few yards towards her, he lifted her onto his shoulder and staggered back up the beach, to where he could see an opening of sorts in the rock face. It seemed to be some sort of natural cave and he laid Martha down on the ground as gently as he could, then examined her shoulder through her gown. There were no bones sticking out, so it was probably just a sprain, although a painful one, to judge by the way she had winced when he touched it. He sank back onto the sandy rock beneath them, regaining his breath.

'Once again, my knight in shining armour to the rescue,' Martha said without a trace of any Irish accent. Daniel simply grunted and when Martha leaned over to kiss him, he rolled away with an expression of displeasure tinged with disgust. There was a long and awkward silence before Martha spoke again. 'George told you, didn't he?'

'Yes,' Daniel replied bluntly, keeping his eyes firmly on the rock above his head. There was another awkward silence, then

Martha reached out a hand and place it on Daniel's chest in a comforting gesture. Daniel brushed the hand away and Martha sighed heavily.

'I'm sorry,' she said.

'Sorry for what, precisely?' Daniel replied bitterly. 'Sorry for misleading an officer of His Majesty's marines in order to acquire better conditions, or sorry for pretending to be Irish?'

'Both, I suppose.'

'I'll give you this much,' Daniel conceded, 'you were very convincing. Had me fooled anyway — perhaps you should have continued your stage career, instead of stooping to theft and false pretences. Anyway, I've learned my lesson.'

'Daniel, please,' Martha begged him, a trembling tear in her voice. 'Let me explain the whole story to you, then perhaps you won't be so angry with me.'

'More of your skilful lies?' Daniel asked, the hurt still evident in his tone.

Martha sighed again. 'I concede that I'm a very good actress and that I had you fooled. But that was only the way it began — since then, believe me, no one's regretted my deception more than I have.'

'Because you got caught out, you mean?'

'Are you going to listen to me or not?' Martha asked, now obviously a little annoyed by his ongoing coldness and cynicism.

'We've got nothing better to do while this storm's raging,' Daniel replied, 'so you might as well relieve the boredom with another of your stories. But please spare me the Irish accent.'

'Gorblimey, guv'nor,' Martha fired back in a perfect imitation of a Cockney barrow boy, 'does yer want the trufe, or sumfink else?'

'Spare me *all* the theatricals,' Daniel replied, although he couldn't hold back the smile at her talent for impersonation, 'just tell me the truth insofar as you're capable. For a start, I take it you *did* steal that comb? Pickpocketing is another of your specialities, is it not?'

'It was *my* comb, originally,' Martha explained. 'That woman on the deck of the ship who was calling me a lying — well, a liar anyway — stole it from me in the first place, on the journey down to Portsmouth from Newgate Gaol. She and two other women held me down while she took it from me, then it was booked in as her property once we got on board the ship and it took me until that morning to get the opportunity to take it back off her, while she was dancing on deck and it fell from her head.'

'But you didn't have the comb on you when they searched you.'

'Didn't I?'

'Well, *did* you?'

'Of course — it was hidden between folds of my long hair. Those old biddies only searched my clothing.'

'Ever the skilful pickpocket with swift hands,' Daniel observed with a lingering trace of censure. 'If you're such a good actress, why did you need to resort to thieving?'

'Do you want the whole story, or simply Mary Murphy's likely version of it?'

'We're obviously here for a while,' Daniel replied, 'and since we're not likely to be talking again in the natural course of events, perhaps I'll choose the whole story.'

'Well, it was like this,' Martha continued in a clear, musical voice that was just as entrancing as her Irish lilt, Daniel couldn't help thinking as he listened, spellbound, to a voice he could happily listen to forever, 'I was born in Trowbridge —

that's in Wiltshire — where my father owned a successful business making textile machinery. "Mallett and Price", it was called and I grew up with all the luxuries you'd expect of a spoiled only child in a successful middle-class family. Then Matthew Price took up with a wicked woman he'd met in Birmingham and made off with all the money. The last we heard, he was somewhere in Holland with all his ill-gotten gains and Father never recovered from the shock of the betrayal and the reversal of business fortunes. He hanged himself one evening and left me to find the body. Mother remarried and my stepfather only seemed interested in feeling me up, so I ran away.'

'And the theatre?' Daniel prompted her.

'That was the easy bit, in one sense,' Martha replied, her eyes glazed into the middle distance as she sat propped up against the wall of the small cave they were sheltering in. 'I'd always had a talent for different voices and I used to keep my school friends in stitches imitating our teachers — even the male ones. So I decided to try my hand at acting in a proper theatre, but soon learned that the only way to succeed as an actress is to act the whore with theatre managers. That part of Mary Murphy was true at least, should you be at all interested — I'm still a virgin.'

'And the thieving?' Daniel demanded.

Martha looked down at him sadly. 'Must you be so judgmental *all* the time? I was a girl of just twenty, all alone in London, with nowhere to go and no one to turn to. Even the lowest flophouses cost money and I needed to eat. I could have sold my body for quite a sum, to judge by some of the offers I'd already received from so-called 'gentlemen', but I wasn't prepared to sink so low. Somehow it was only too easy to use my talent for being someone else in order to sneakthieve things I could sell. My best regular performance was probably the sweet old lady begging in the gutter — when fine gentlemen stopped to give me a conscience-soothing penny, I could palm their purses or their gold watches with the best of them.'

'Presumably it wasn't an old lady who deprived a bishop of his drawers?' Daniel asked, now completely fascinated by the tale she had to tell, whether it was more lies or not.

Martha giggled. 'My finest achievement, they tell me, although it got me sent out here. There's obviously no resale value in a clergyman's underpants, but I did it for a wager with another pickpocket I shared a bed with in a flophouse in Shoreditch. She liked to think of herself as the best "dip" in the trade and she dared me to come back to the house with a pair of under-drawers bearing the name of a clergyman sewn into its label. Round the corner from where we stayed was a convent and the nuns were obviously taking in washing. I followed several of them until I found them calling regularly at a big house in Clerkenwell, where an old man dressed like a clergyman often came to the door. So, dressed as a nun, I called at the house one day and the housekeeper came out. I told her that we thought there'd been a mix-up with laundry from another clergyman and could she possibly search in the washing basket that had come from the convent the previous day? When she brought the basket to the door, I was fortunate enough to find the drawers in them, grabbed them and ran off. The housekeeper called in the constables and since the sight of a nun in full flight carrying the drawers of a bishop is not an everyday occurrence in the streets of North London, I was soon spotted and you know the rest.'

Despite himself, Daniel burst out laughing. He wiped a tear from his eye and noticed that Martha was doing the same.

Then he realised that hers were not caused by laughter and he stopped laughing and reached out a consoling hand. Martha grabbed it with both hands and kissed it fervently several times before she composed herself and continued.

'Funny though that exploit was, it was what led me out here. I honest to God thought I was going to be hanged, but I batted my eyelids at the old misery who was the judge at my trial and he decided that my life was to be spared. There are days when I wish he hadn't.'

'It's not much fun out here, I agree,' Daniel said. 'In fact, earlier today I made my mind up to go back on the next vessel sailing for England on which they have a passage for a marine lieutenant.'

A look of fear crossed Martha's face. 'No!' she cried.

Daniel looked up and across to where she was sitting. 'Why should you care?' he asked, curiosity blending with hope.

Martha seemed about to blurt out something else, but she bit her lip and thought for a moment before replying. 'You're a good man,' she said. 'There aren't so many around like you and this colony is going to need all the good men it can get, if it is to become something other than a prison camp by the sea.'

'I do the job for which I was commissioned,' Daniel replied with resignation. 'I'm surely not the only one who does that.'

'But you do it without exploiting others,' Martha pointed out. 'Believe me, I know what I'm talking about. I know I have good looks, but they've been nothing but a handicap in my dealings with men. Of course I've used them for my own ends...'

'Like pretending to be Mary Murphy and seducing an officer of His Majesty's marines into giving you preference,' he interrupted her. 'When we first met, you were one of over a hundred transported criminals in the stinking hold of a rat-infested convict ship. Now you're a nursemaid to a family that will grow in prestige and preferment, given George Johnston's obvious ambition, and in due course you'll no doubt be married to money and power. Not bad for a Shoreditch pickpocket. Tick me off as another of your dupes,' he added bitterly.

'If you had let me finish,' she persevered, 'I was going to tell you just how true a gentleman you are. May I finish what I need to say, before you go off again?'

'Continue,' Daniel said, lowering himself back down off his elbow to continue studying the rock ceiling.

'I admit that to begin with I used you,' Martha continued. 'I thought you just saw me as a pretty Irish girl with a good body and a wayward girlish charm. That continued until the evening you came back and told me that you could arrange for me to go ashore and live in peace from those who were persecuting me. When I climbed under that canvas with you, I was expecting to have to finally pay the price with my long-preserved virginity. But you just held me in your arms as if I was someone special and you showed me genuine affection rather than lust. After you fell asleep, I cried in your arms until I fell asleep myself. I'd finally found someone who saw more in me. So don't try and pretend that you're not something special, because you are.'

Daniel could stand it no longer. He was being dragged down a lovely dark tunnel that could only have one possible ending and he had to escape while he still had command of his very soul. 'You *really* should have become an actress,' he said as he rose to his feet and looked across the bay. 'The storm's over now — you go back to your world and leave me in mine.' He strode determinedly back towards his tent.

4

A week or so later, Captain Shea died from the illness that had laid him low ever since the fleet had landed and which everyone was praying had not been cholera. His burial was swift, with all the officers of his regiment ordered to the graveside while the colony's chaplain, the Reverend Richard Johnson, read the fastest burial service that was humanly possible, as if apprehensive that even the ground into which the body had been consigned in a naval canvas shroud might itself be infected.

'It's an ill wind,' George Johnston said as he pinned the new captain's regalia onto his red frock coat, standing on the veranda outside the governor's house on which the officers of the Marine Corps had been paraded in order to learn of the resulting promotions. Major Ross had not unduly taxed his brain in the choice of replacements, simply moving everyone up in the order of their seniority. George was now Captain Johnston and Daniel was a First Lieutenant, thanks to George's patronage.

By the time that the governor's fine sandstone mansion was ready for his occupation, the colony was in serious difficulties. Every officer had been ordered to open up a small garden adjacent to their hut and almost all of them had reported the same crop failure. Those who had sown seeds brought from the Cape had the satisfaction of watching green shoots spring up from the ground, only to wither, turn yellow and die under the remorseless sun. Those who had planted English seed didn't even have the satisfaction of seeing early shoots and all attempts at plant cultivation were abandoned in the beach area

— including in the governor's own private garden — when it was deduced that the seed they had brought with them would not grow in sand without some heavy manure, of which there was virtually none.

One result of this agricultural experiment had been to force Daniel into a hut, which he shared with another lieutenant and two privates. He had deliberately chosen one on the 'Rocks' side of the cove, in order to be as far away as possible from where Martha was living and he had managed to exchange duties so that he no longer had to walk past their hut twice daily. He was now in command of the prison brig hut and was also on permanent standby for any action that might be required in response to attacks from the natives.

The natives, for their part, had not come any closer to the settlement than the foliage surrounding it, which was now about a mile back from the shore as the simple colony slowly expanded. The quarry that Daniel had once guarded was now a brick works anyway and most of the timber from the first forest area had been felled, requiring teams of convicts to move further and further out from the safety of the main settlement and float logs behind ships' cutters from where they had felled them to the south, all the way down to the original landing site at Botany Bay. Here they were more vulnerable to attack from the natives and from time to time the embryonic community in Sydney Cove would learn that another group of convict forestry workers had been attacked and killed, or had been dragged into the 'bushland' and never seen again. Whenever marines were sent to protect the convicts the natives seemed to keep their distance and it was not long before no one was allowed beyond a mile from the foreshore without a military escort.

The result of all the tree felling, house construction and quarrying had been a need for new tools, as old ones became blunt, or damaged beyond repair. Two former blacksmiths had been ordered to open and operate a forge, but there was little metal to be had and everyone waited anxiously for the Second Fleet that had been promised. Every day lookouts were posted on the 'South Head' of the long estuary that led from the ocean opening into the broad sheltered cove for sight of approaching sails. When they didn't come, the *Sirius* was sent back to the Cape to purchase supplies with what little money was left.

It was rapidly becoming apparent that the only realistic prospect of a sufficient crop to feed the growing Port Jackson colony lay inland, along the banks of the many inlets that ran west from the Cove, which had their origins in freshwater streams and ran through more fertile-looking land. Within the first year, only one man had succeeded in growing wheat within the immediate environs of Port Jackson and while it was not an adequate crop to feed the entire colony, it demonstrated the man's obvious talents as a farmer. His name was James Ruse and he had farmed land in Cornwall before being transported for burglary.

Upon learning of the man's talents, Governor Phillip arranged for him to travel inland to an area that he had already identified and named 'Rose Hill'. It was some fifteen miles inland from Port Jackson, along a wide saltwater tributary that wound its way west until it opened out into a fertile valley through which fresh water flowed. There was a defensible hill called 'The Crescent' upon which a military garrison could be stationed and Phillip had ambitions to expand the entire area into a second colony, if it could be made to sustain a sizeable population. Phillip lost no time in sending Ruse out west to

44

Rose Hill, to develop an experimental farm and with him went a detachment of marines led by Daniel, who was glad to be free of the constraints of Sydney Cove and the ever-present possibility of crossing paths with Martha. However, his orders were to establish the garrison, then leave it to others to man it.

Upon his return Daniel was met by a very aggrieved George Johnston, who insisted that Daniel accompany him to the waterfront, where a massive wharf had now been built at which smaller vessels could load and unload people and supplies, should any arrive. George pointed down at the wharf, where a queue of people had formed.

'See there?' George said. 'That's the *Charlotte* — she's setting sail for China today and the *Lady Penrhyn* and *Scarborough* go tomorrow.'

'So?' Daniel asked. 'We knew they would leave eventually.'

'Take a closer look at that woman sitting on the bollard next to that wagon.'

Daniel peered more carefully and there was no mistaking the long black hair flowing out from under the bonnet. 'It's Martha, clearly — so what?'

'She's been sitting there every day for a week,' George complained. 'She seems to be terrified that you're planning to leave without her and we haven't been able to get any work out of her. I tried to convince her that you were out west at the new garrison, but she accused me of covering for you while you slipped away without her. What in God's name did you promise her?'

'Nothing,' Daniel insisted. 'I told her that I was seeking a passage back to England but I haven't made my wishes known to the governor yet. I made Martha no promise that she could come with me — I could never trust another woman to play true with my heart, and in any case a woman with her background would be completely unacceptable in English society.'

'For God's sake, man,' George remonstrated with him, 'your prospects of a return passage are *very* remote, let me assure you. For one thing, you're too highly thought of here. For another, there are very few berths for non-paying passengers on any voyage back to Portsmouth. And thirdly — and most importantly, to my mind — you have a happy future mapped out for you here, with a respected position, a society free of the sort of social divisions that made Martha an outcast in the first place, and a willing and beautiful woman who worships the boots on your feet.'

'I don't want worship, George,' Daniel told him, 'simply a safe reception for my love and devotion. But I'll go and reassure Martha that I'm not leaving just yet, then perhaps she'll resume her duties.'

Daniel walked down to where Martha was sitting, musing over what George had said. She was certainly beautiful, but it was her lively personality that held him entranced. But he could not risk the agony of being rejected, or — even worse — being cuckolded after they had married. Daniel knew that his heart could not take the constant worry of being the ageing spouse of a beautiful woman.

She looked up as he walked over and a wide smile of relief lit up her face.

Daniel nodded towards the *Charlotte*, where people and baggage were being hauled over the gunnels. 'Did you think I was leaving on her?'

Martha nodded.

'I *may* leave one day, as I told you. But I'll be sure to let you know when that day comes — *if* it comes.'

Martha reached out and grasped his hand. 'If it does, I would also like to be on the passenger list.'

'Any woman who goes back to England with me would have to be Mrs. Bradbury.'

'Is that an offer?' Martha asked eagerly.

'No, it is not,' Daniel told her. 'But I feel sure that with your looks, your charm and your ability to be whatever someone wants you to be, you'll have no shortage of other offers.'

'Funny you should mention that,' Martha replied with a hardened expression. 'There's a young private in George's detachment who leaves me in no doubt that he'd like to make an honest woman of me. Name of "Perkin" — you should take care that you don't get too high and mighty, else I might take him up on his offer. Just make sure you don't wait too long for the *right* woman!'

With that she bristled off back up the beach, leaving Daniel lost for words, but in a sense less troubled in his mind, in the belief that he'd finally driven her away from where she could torment his indecision.

5

Esther's baby — a boy — was born in late October. They called him George Junior and a celebration party was organised for one evening in the second week following the birth. The invitees consisted principally of marines, naval officers and the governor and his staff, and Daniel did not feel he could politely refuse, even though it would mean another uncomfortable meeting with Martha, in a very confined space in which they would be obliged to make polite conversation. But as it transpired it was a balmy dry evening and once the sun dipped behind the range of hills to the south-west the party moved out into the failed garden immediately in front of the cramped hut. Daniel had delayed turning up until the last moment consistent with good manners and by the time he got there, the party was in full swing.

Martha lost no time in walking over the coarse sandy grass towards him on the arm of a marine private, who replaced the black tricorn hat on his short ginger hair when he realised that he was about to be introduced to an officer. He saluted as they stood before each other, the younger man squaring the broadest pair of shoulders Daniel had ever seen inside a red tunic.

'Daniel,' Martha announced, 'I imagine that you know Private Perkin.'

The young man leaned down from well over six feet in height to shake Daniel's hand as if determined to crush the circulation out of it.

'Pleased to meet you, sir,' he said. 'Edward Perkin. I don't believe we've actually spoken before. I was on the *Scarborough* on the way out, and I gather that you were on the *Lady Penrhyn*.'

'Yes indeed, as was Miss Mallett here,' Daniel told him with a feeling of malicious satisfaction, in case Martha had tried to adopt another persona in order to charm her admirer. 'What detail are you on out here?'

'Commissary Store guard, sir,' Perkin replied.

'The job obviously has its advantages,' Martha chipped in. 'Edward was able to bring a huge jug of rum to keep the party going. Plus a pound of pouch tobacco for George's pipe.'

Edward blushed slightly and Daniel wondered if it was from embarrassment or guilt. As if being called upon to explain himself, Edward added, 'I don't drink or smoke myself, sir, so I'm able to save most of my pay and some of the other men are quite happy to part with their rations as well, so...'

'Yes, quite,' Daniel replied, making a mental note to enquire who else was selling illicit grog and tobacco around the colony. Just then a fiddler struck up a reel and a group of men and their ladies began to form a square on the grass.

'Come on, Edward,' Martha said, with a backward look at Daniel that was a mixture of triumph and challenge, 'they need another couple to make up their eight.'

They hurried off towards the dancers and Daniel made his way indoors, where Esther was sitting proudly behind a box that contained a conglomeration of blankets and sheets, inside which was presumably the newborn whose arrival they were here to celebrate. She looked for all the world like a street trader selling vegetables at a Saturday market.

Daniel walked over and placed a gold coin down on the table that was set up to one side for the presents. He hoped that Esther would realise that the gift was traditional and not a simple admission that he had no imagination and no experience of gifting newborns. She smiled at him encouragingly and Daniel could see why George had fallen for her. She had a long, serious, face but there was a burning intelligence in her dark eyes.

'So nice to renew our acquaintance again in happier circumstances, Daniel,' she said. 'George speaks very highly of you, as, of course, does Martha. Thank you again for finding her for us.' Esther looked through the open door towards the dancers. 'Martha's trying to make you jealous, dancing with Perkin.'

'Why would she think I'd be jealous?' Daniel asked in the most neutral tone of voice he could summon, although he could feel his pulse quickening even at the mere mention of Martha's name.

'Please don't underestimate a woman's instinct,' Esther replied. 'You and she have been walking around each other like two prize-fighters in the ring ever since we landed. You're obviously strongly attracted to each other, but from what Martha tells me you're reluctant to commit to a relationship.'

'She talks about me, does she?' Daniel asked.

'She talks about nothing *else*,' Esther chortled back. 'There are times I feel I know you very well, the way she prattles on about you. Please don't break her heart, Daniel — she's too dear to me already.'

'It's *my* heart I'm concerned for,' Daniel replied, unable to withstand the strong urge to unburden himself to someone who might have the life experience to understand. 'I was cruelly deceived once before, you see.'

'Did she deceive you, or did you deceive *yourself*?' Esther asked with a serious look in her eye.

Daniel looked away in surprise — he'd never thought of it that way. 'I allowed myself to believe that she loved me, certainly,' he admitted. 'Her name was Alice and she was my employer's older daughter. She always smiled when we met and we used to joke happily between ourselves, so naturally I thought...'

The rest of what he might have said was drowned by a snort from Esther. 'Typical male conceit! A few smiles, the odd joke here and there and she's all yours for the asking? Women look for more than that in a man, let me tell you. A loving heart certainly. A sense of humour a bonus. But unless they feel in their inner being that this is the person they want for the father of their babies, it's all just politeness and pretence. When I first laid eyes on George, even though he was strutting up and down the gangway between messes and I was one of the pieces of dirt lying to one side of him, I knew. He looked twice at me and I think *he* knew as well.'

Two naval officers walked into the hut with their women on their arms. The women twitted and cooed over the baby and Esther reverted to her proud mother role. As Daniel started to move away, she grabbed his sleeve and pulled him down until his ear was level with her mouth. 'Please don't fight it too hard, Daniel,' she whispered. 'You have to learn to trust again, otherwise you'll *both* lose something very precious.'

Daniel's head was reeling as he walked outside, where the warm, slightly humid, air did nothing to clear his thoughts. The dance had now become a waltz and Daniel yearned to interrupt Martha and her escort as they swirled around, crush her in his arms and surrender. He'd been burned once, but he longed to get burned again.

6

A week later, Daniel was obliged to take a patrol of marines up to the brickworks in a show of military might, to deter any more attacks from natives that seemed to be aimed at stealing tools. They were marching past George's hut when George himself walked from his front step into the broad sunlight and ordered a halt. He called Daniel over.

'The governor doesn't want to provoke any mass attacks while our powder reserves are so low, so don't let anyone shoot the natives.'

'What about Major Ross's orders?' Daniel asked, relieved at this new instruction.

'Ignore them,' George insisted. 'The governor was very clear.'

Daniel continued to march with his men up the long slope and through the dense bushland that marked the western fringe of the first forest that had been felled. The brickworks were still half a mile or so further on when Daniel raised his hand in a signal for the entire platoon to halt. Ahead of them was a native boy, perhaps no more than fifteen, sitting in an open space between two tall gum trees, playing with what looked like a hammer and chisel. It had presumably been stolen from the brickworks to which they were heading and Daniel whispered an order to his half dozen or so privates to fix bayonets, along with a stern instruction that there was to be no firing of muskets. He also ordered them to remain where they were.

He walked slowly up to where the youth sat, seemingly unconcerned at the approach of soldiers and Daniel suspected a trap. He looked around cautiously, but there was no sign of any other native, so he walked up to the youth and bent down to enquire, in the most simple language he could summon up, where he had come across the tools he was playing with. Suddenly there was a warning shout from one of his men and he felt a massive blow to the side of his head as a tall man sprang out from behind a wide tree trunk and felled him.

When he came round a few moments later, he was surrounded by natives, all pointing their spears at him. He looked back to where his own men stood, silent and uncertain and yelled an order: 'No firing! Conserve your powder!'

He looked back up at a ring of threatening faces and prepared himself for a painful death. Then there was a shout and a young warrior pushed his way to the front. He studied Daniel for a moment, then broke into a grin. He reached out his hand and pulled Daniel to his feet, murmuring, 'Friend.'

Daniel felt a rush of relief as he realised that this must be the boy whose life he had spared months before. There was an animated conversation between the man who had pulled Daniel to his feet — who was presumably the leader of this raiding party — and the rest of the group. The leader waved a hand towards where Daniel's men were standing, awestricken, their muskets at their shoulders in the firing position and asked, 'Friend?'

Daniel nodded and held out an open hand as he gestured back to his men. 'Friends. All friends.'

'We could pot every one of them from here, sir,' shouted one private. 'They've only got spears and we're all loaded and ready.'

'Back away, Private,' Daniel ordered him. '*All* of you, back away quietly. Anyone who fires will be on a charge.'

The marine contingent walked slowly backwards, their weapons loosely by their sides and the natives melted into the bush as if they were part of it. Daniel dusted off his uniform tunic and ordered the men to continue the march to the brickworks.

Two days later, Daniel was in irons inside the brig hut that he had been guarding for some months. The charge was 'cowardice in the face of the enemy' and Major Ross was determined to make his point. The court martial had been set for a week's time and Daniel was to be defended by none other than his own immediate senior officer, George Johnston. The 'prosecution' was in the hands of Second Lieutenant William Bray, who hoped to become a first lieutenant when the man who was standing in the way of his promotion was taken out onto the parade square and shot.

George had gloomily told Daniel that none of the men who had been under his command during the incident was prepared to say anything other than that they were simply following orders when Daniel had bartered for his life when they could easily have killed half a dozen natives. Major Ross was apparently incandescent when he learned that an opportunity had been missed to show the natives that the settlers could wipe them out and was determined to make an example of a senior officer who had backed away from such a show of force in order to save his own life. And yet somehow George seemed quietly confident that he could get Daniel off the charge and assured him that 'a truth of sorts' would emerge.

On the day of his court martial, Daniel was marched smartly into the room in the recently completed courthouse that the military had commandeered for the occasion. He groaned inwardly when he looked up and saw Major Ross himself seated at the centre of the judge's table, a senior naval officer on either side of him.

The charge was read out and Daniel indignantly denied cowardice. Then, one by one, the men who had been with him on that day testified.

George then stood up to begin his opening speech for the defence. 'Gentlemen, I have to begin by expressing a difficulty I have in this matter. Certain pertinent facts that will support the prisoner's defence are known only to me and as you are aware, I cannot give evidence for myself whilst acting as "prisoner's friend" in this matter. However, I hope that you will grant me a certain indulgence if on occasions I ask questions to which I obviously know the answer, because I am referring to conversations in which I took part. I call my first witness — the prisoner.'

Daniel was not allowed to move from his seat into the witness box, so George adopted a position across the courtroom from which to ask his questions, far enough away to justify the loud voice in which he asked them, determined that the judges should not miss a word.

He began by taking Daniel through the sequence of events once the platoon had come across the native boy with the apparently stolen tools. When Daniel recalled how the leader of the native group had hauled him to his feet and called him 'Friend', George asked him to explain how they knew each other and Daniel obligingly recalled the previous incident when he had prevented the man from being killed.

'So this was the *second* time you'd saved the life of the same ignorant savage?' Major Ross interrupted indignantly.

Daniel stared him back defiantly as he responded. 'On the first occasion, it would have been wanton slaughter. Added to which, we had no way of knowing how many other natives were hiding in the trees and we could have been risking our own lives, had we taken his.'

'So once again, your primary concern was for your own neck?' Ross observed triumphantly.

'The lives of my own men as well, sir. It is surely an officer's duty to preserve the lives of his own men.'

'He has a point, Ross,' one of the naval judges remarked. Ross let the matter drop and nodded grumpily for George to continue his examination-in-chief.

'Before you recommenced the march, after you left my hut, had you been given any new order?'

'I had been told that the governor wished to conserve our powder, certainly. Any deaths were to be by bayonet and only *then* if we were under attack.'

'And from whom did you receive that order?'

'You — *sir*,' Daniel replied, a little discomforted.

'And at the time when you were lifted from the ground by the native, would it have been possible for your men to rescue you?'

'Only if they had opened fire with their muskets.'

'No chance of attacking them with bayonets?'

'Definitely not — they were some ten feet away at that time.'

'And you were not, at that moment, under attack in any way?'

'No — if anything, the entire situation had been defused.'

George indicated that he had no further questions.

Lieutenant Bray rose with the glint of triumph in his eyes. 'This entire incident took place on the 23rd?'

'Correct,' Daniel replied.

'And you say that you received the order concerning the conservation of powder earlier that morning, before the incident?'

'Yes.'

'Then how do you explain the fact that this order did not come into force until the *following* day, when Major Ross had it announced at General Parade?'

'Obviously I can't, but I was receiving an order from *my* superior officer and as you are no doubt aware, he's the governor's adjutant. I was told that the order came from the governor himself.'

There was a snort of indignation from Major Ross, who waved his hand for Lieutenant Bray to remain silent for a moment, while he bellowed down the courtroom, 'Who is your *ultimate* commanding officer, Lieutenant?'

'You are, sir.'

'But you claim to have obeyed an order from the governor. Is that not in itself an act of insubordination?'

'With respect, sir,' Daniel replied heatedly, 'I obeyed an order from *my* immediate superior officer. If men were allowed to conduct their own enquiries before satisfying themselves that an order from a superior officer is an authorised one, it would be chaos. I have been trained to obey orders from a superior officer and it's none of my business if the governor issues an order to his adjutant before he gets round to telling you.'

There was a roar of laughter around the courtroom, led by the two naval officers on either side of Ross, who were well aware of the war being waged between the governor and his commanding officer. Ross glared at Daniel, but said nothing more and Lieutenant Bray sat down in confusion. George had been hastily scribbling a note on a piece of paper, which he handed to one of the privates guarding the courtroom door. The guard saluted and hurried outside and George turned to address the bench.

'I call Miss Martha Mallett.'

Daniel's heart performed its usual somersault as he saw Martha being ushered into the courtroom and almost fainted with shock when she scuttled over to him on her way to the witness box and planted a big warm kiss on his mouth. 'That's fer you, darlin',' she said loudly as she stepped into the witness box and declined to take the oath on the ground that she was of the Jewish faith.

Daniel swiftly forgot that he was on trial for his life as he listened in rapt fascination to the performance that Martha was giving, posing as a simple Cockney girl.

'Miss Mallett,' George asked her, 'you seem very familiar with the defendant, judging by the kiss you just gave him.'

'Yeah, that's right. I've give 'im more than a kiss, many's the time.'

'At the risk of embarrassing you, Miss Mallett, could you explain precisely what you meant by that last answer?' George asked, with a warning look towards Daniel.

'Who's embarrassed? I'm not, an' that's the honest truth. 'E's 'ad me body more than once.'

There was a warning cough from the bench and George did his best to look embarrassed. 'Do you mean to say that you and Lieutenant Bradbury here are lovers?'

'Well, I love it, darlin', an' ter judge be the way 'e goes at it, 'e loves it an' all.'

It was all Daniel could do to keep a straight face and he was glad that he had been pre-warned by George to keep his mouth firmly shut. Instead, he just sat back and enjoyed the performance.

'Miss Mallett, on the 23rd of last month, did you have any conversations with the lieutenant?'

'Yeah — we arranged ter meet in the forest fer you know wot.'

The two naval officers were almost drooling as they looked down the brazen cleavage of Martha's dress, which she had spent two whole days stretching so that when she pulled it forward in pretended agitation, as if seeking to cool herself, it revealed the deliciously rounded tops of her more than ample breasts. Major Ross, for his part, looked somewhat nonplussed as to where all this was leading and kept his eyes firmly on Daniel.

'As I understand it, Miss Mallett,' George persevered, 'you're telling us that you and the lieutenant arranged a liaison in the forest?'

'Yeah — we agreed as 'ow 'e were gonna take 'is men up the road ter the brickworks, then nip back an' meet me in the trees.'

'Did you follow the column of men into the forest?'

'Yeah, but I kept myself well 'idden, which was p'raps as well, as it turned out.'

'How exactly *did* it "turn out", Miss Mallett?'

'Well, it were like this,' Martha replied, staring hard at the far wall with a fixed expression, as if reliving the event in her mind, 'I were followin' the soldiers, but stickin' ter the trees. Me an' Danny, we 'as our own special place, in a clearin' near where the stream runs down ter the beach. I were sittin' there, waitin' fer Danny ter come back, when I sees all these blokes wanderin' through the trees, carryin' spears. I were proper scared, so I lay down an' 'id meself. Then I 'eard Danny shout and the next thing I knows, there 'e is on the ground, wiv this bloke pullin' 'im to 'is feet, an' all these other blokes in the bushes, lookin' on, like they was waitin' ter see what 'appened next.'

'If I might stop you right there, Miss Mallett,' George said, 'could you tell me approximately how many native men were watching what was going on from the surrounding bushes?'

Martha seemed to think for a moment, then answered, 'About fifty, I reckon.'

'Did they seem to be in a position to attack the marine detachment, if any of them had started firing?'

'Not 'alf. I don't think Danny an' 'is men coulda known they was there, an' if our blokes 'ad started firin' or anyfin, theyd've bin done ter death by all the men wiv spears what was 'idin' in the bushes.'

'Thank you, Miss Mallett,' George said as he sat down, with a sly grin across towards where Daniel was sitting, as straight-faced as he could manage in the circumstances.

Lieutenant Bray rose and regarded Martha as if someone had just dangled a long-dead rat under his nose. 'You don't deny that you and Lieutenant Bradbury here are, or have been, in a sexual relationship?'

'No, 'course not,' Martha replied proudly.

'And some might say that you've only come here today to save him from the firing squad.'

'They'd be right, an' all,' Martha countered. 'Why should 'e get shot fer cowardice, when 'e saved 'is entire troop from gettin' speared ter death?'

At this point, Bray wisely sat down and George stood up again, having just been slipped a note by one of the guards. 'I have one final witness, who should perhaps not be kept waiting any longer than necessary. I call the governor of New South Wales.'

There were gasps of amazement as Governor Phillip strode in, bowed slightly to the judges and walked swiftly to the witness box. Daniel groaned inwardly in the belief that George was pushing his luck, but like everyone else he was agog to know what the governor could add to the proceedings. George took him quickly through the preliminaries, then went for the main point. 'Could you tell the court whether or not, on the 23rd March last, you issued an instruction regarding the preservation of powder in the Commissary Store?'

'Indeed I did,' Governor Phillip replied. 'As you will know, supplies of all descriptions are running low and I have a particular interest in maintaining peaceful relations with the natives whose land we've invaded, so I issued an order that the natives were not to be fired on with musket balls and were only to be bayoneted if there was no other way of preserving the lives of the colonists.'

'And to whom did you give that order?'

'I gave it to you, Captain, as my adjutant.'

'Not to Major Ross first?'

'I issued the same order to Major Ross, but as usual he seemed to regard an order from the governor as somewhat low on his list of priorities. I was anxious that the order should go down the ranks as quickly as possible, so I gave the order to you, knowing that you would lose no time in informing the marines of my wishes.'

'So your order was to be carried out that day?'

'Indeed.'

'Thank you, Governor,' George replied. 'One more question, if I may, then hopefully we can allow you to resume your normal duties. I realise that your military experience has been largely naval in nature, but what would be your opinion of a soldier who deliberately defuses a situation in which his men are surrounded by the enemy, in circumstances in which that enemy could wipe out all his men and who manages to bring the entire crisis to a halt by placing his own life in jeopardy?'

'I would regard that man as a hero, why?'

It went deathly quiet, until one of the naval officers coughed politely and said, 'That's in effect what this man is accused of, Governor.'

'What, saving his men by putting his own life on the line?'

'Yes, Governor,' the naval man replied with a sideways look at Major Ross. 'It seems that the prisoner had some prior acquaintance with the leader of a native group and was actually able to shake hands with him in a manoeuvre that saved his men from being slaughtered where they stood.'

The governor's eyes widened in disbelief. 'And that's what he's being court martialled for? Is this your doing, Ross?'

'I was simply observing normal procedure, following a report of cowardice in the face of the enemy,' Ross explained.

'They are not *yet* the enemy, Major Ross, but they are more likely to become that if you discipline men who are clearly capable of making friends with them. If this man is found guilty, you'll answer to me — is that understood?'

Ross nodded and Lieutenant Bray stood up for long enough to announce that he had no questions to ask the governor, then sat down as if about to hide under the table.

The court found Daniel not guilty without even having to withdraw to consider the matter.

7

The next day, while Daniel was lying on his cot bed in his hut, thinking how much he owed to Martha, a private knocked on the door and told him that Governor Phillip wished to see him immediately. Daniel put on his best dress jacket, polished his boots with the old rag he kept for the purpose, decided that a shave would take too long and marched smartly down to Governor's Mansion, the new stone one that had been in use for several weeks.

'Sit down, man, and have a glass of brandy,' Governor Phillip invited him.

As Daniel savoured the smooth burning taste of the first strong liquor he'd tasted for weeks, Governor Phillip came straight to the point.

'Let's get down to business, Lieutenant. George Johnston gave me the full inside story behind your experience up by the brickworks and he also told me the truth about Miss Mallett's part in securing your acquittal.'

'With respect, Governor,' Daniel ventured to interrupt, 'it was, I believe, *your* intervention that saved my neck.'

'A neck that should never have been at risk in the first place, if that damned stuffed-shirt Ross knew his business. That remark goes no further than this room, understood?'

Daniel nodded and Governor Phillip continued.

'I meant every word of what I said at your court martial. To be perfectly candid with you — and this goes no further either, by the way — we've got our arses hanging out of the window in this colony, the way things are at present. The supplies are running low at an alarming rate, the crops in the main don't seem to thrive, the few animals we brought with us are running out of fodder and the food supplies are getting critical. The last thing we need is natives attacking us — in fact, we need to establish friendly relations with them, in the hope that they can teach us how to survive in this weird bloody place.'

'How do you think I may be able to help? That's why you asked to see me, I assume?'

'That and congratulating you for your bravery in saving your men. But it's how you did it that fascinates me. You and this native fellow actually shook hands?'

'Yes. The first time we met, we had him at our mercy, but I opted to let him go. I took his hand and called him "friend". When he had me at *his* mercy near the brickworks, he did exactly the same for me, even repeating the word "friend".'

'He remembered the word?' Governor Phillip asked, intrigued.

'Yes, sir.'

'That proves that they can learn English. If they'd stop running away from us for long enough, we could maybe teach them enough English for them to help us. God knows, if we don't see that fleet we were promised by London before much longer, we'll all be dead from starvation anyway, so I don't really see that we have much choice but to befriend the locals.'

'And I'm the only man you know of who's actually spoken to one of them?' Daniel asked.

'Precisely. You've obviously earned the man's respect and his tribe will apparently do what he tells them. You're our best bet for making peaceful contact with these people.'

Daniel looked doubtful.

'This Mallett woman who lied through her teeth for you — and, incidentally, made a considerable impression on Captain Tait — she's your woman?' Governor Phillip asked.

'No, not exactly,' Daniel admitted. 'I was able to preserve her from some of the worst of the brutality on the *Lady Penrhyn* and I got her that position with George Johnston, so no doubt she felt she owed me something. And her performance was spellbinding — she's nothing *like* the common Londoner she pretended to be for the benefit of the court. She's actually quite well spoken and surprisingly intelligent for a convict woman.'

'You know she's out here for offences of dishonesty, of course?'

'Yes, but she's somehow managed to explain that all in a way that's quite convincing. But then again, she's a skilled actress with convictions for fraud, so she ought to be a very plausible confidence trickster.'

'Just watching your face while you talk about her suggests to me that you're very fond of her,' Governor Phillip observed.

'Yes, I am — but we're not in any sort of relationship other than one of mutual attraction.'

'Perhaps you should think about improving on that,' Governor Phillip told him. 'If you want to make her your wife — or even your mistress — I can commute her sentence pretty severely. She's out here for seven years, but she's served over two of those, counting back to the date of her first arrest and my powers as governor would allow me to grant her a ticket of leave almost immediately — *if...*'

'If what?' Daniel asked, intrigued.

'If you can bring me in that native you've made contact with, so that we can begin the process of getting to know them and gaining their assistance. Also, if she'll agree to start up a theatre here in Port Jackson. The few ladies we have in the colony are desperate for a little entertainment and some of the officers have suggested a theatre, or something along those lines. As far as I know, Miss Mallett is the only professional performer we have in the colony and we could hardly have our only palace of culture run by a convict woman — we'd be the laughing stock of Whitehall.'

'I'll give it some thought, Governor,' Daniel said as he rose to leave.

'Make it sooner rather than later,' Governor Phillip said as he held out his hand to shake Daniel's. 'The same goes for your relationship with Miss Mallett. Good men like you need resourceful women behind them and the Reverend Johnson was complaining only the other day about how few weddings he's been required to conduct while he's been out here. The colony needs a strong new generation.'

The following evening Daniel changed into the only smart civilian suit he possessed and walked up the slope towards George's cottage to join him for a celebratory dinner. He was almost at the door when Martha appeared, carrying Roseanna in her arms and walking in the opposite direction. She started when she saw Daniel, but slowed down as they drew close to each other and finally stopped in front of him.

'I'm taking Roseanna for some fresh air,' she explained, 'since the air's cooler out here and I gather that the conquering hero's being feted and feasted.'

'Thanks to you, I'm not lying in a military grave,' Daniel said as he leaned forward to kiss her.

She averted her face and pursed her lips in a disapproving grimace. 'I owed you lots of favours, but I think they're probably all repaid now. Consider us equal.'

'Does that mean we can start to get to know each other better?' Daniel asked.

'I rather think not,' Martha huffed. 'George told me that the governor's prepared to grant me my freedom if I marry you — is that what you mean by "getting to know me better"?'

'No,' Daniel protested, 'that's not how it was. Certainly, he's prepared to consider your ticket of leave if certain conditions are fulfilled...'

'Forget it, Daniel!' Martha spat back. 'Marry you in return for my freedom? And what sort of freedom would *that* be? Bought like a prize heifer in a cattle market, eternally grateful to the big strong saviour who released her from bondage? I think I'd rather be the revolting little harlot that I pretended to be to save your neck. Now get out of my way, please!'

She stormed off down the slope, while Daniel stared at her retreating form and asked himself how things could have gone so horribly wrong.

A few minutes later Daniel was sitting outside, sipping dandelion wine and enjoying the last of the evening sun with George and Esther. Daniel had been busily explaining that the governor had asked him personally to acquire the services of the native he'd befriended and bring him into Port Jackson. He had also mentioned the governor's promise to grant Martha her freedom, and Esther had voiced her concern that she might be losing her nursemaid.

'I hardly think you need concern yourself about that,' George assured her. 'Even if she becomes a free woman, she'll still need to work for a living and we can offer her a wage.'

'Not if she marries Daniel,' Esther reminded him, to which Daniel had responded that this now seemed very unlikely.

'In fact, I doubt if she'd be prepared to talk to me civilly, after she got it into her head that marrying me was the price of her freedom.'

'No wonder,' Esther pointed out. 'No woman likes to think that she's been bought and sold without even being consulted. Just fold her in your arms, tell her you love her and ask for her hand in marriage,' Esther told him. 'Women always love a little romance and gallantry and she simply adores you, I know she does.'

Daniel was still thinking about the task ahead of him as he congratulated George on the fish they were eating for dinner. 'Where did it come from, exactly? The governor seems to think that we're on the brink of starvation, but if we can get a ready supply of fish this good, we might contrive to live a little longer.'

'If the natives don't assassinate us first,' George told him. 'We can only go fishing if we take a full complement of armed men with us. This lot came from that bay where we first landed, before the governor opted for Port Jackson. I wasn't there, obviously, but when Private Mullery and his men came back with an entire ship's boat full, he gave me a couple. He told me that they could have got more, but that they had to beat a hasty retreat from the shallows they were trawling nets through when spears started whistling past their ears.'

'So the natives go to Botany Bay to fish?' Daniel asked thoughtfully.

'Apparently,' George confirmed.

'So if I go and sit on the beach with a fishing line, or a net, sooner or later they'll come and attack me?'

'Are you serious?' George demanded, spitting a fish bone onto his plate. 'They won't exactly sit down beside you and ask how the fish are biting — they'll just lob spears at you from the undergrowth.'

'That's a risk I have to take *wherever* I choose to go in order to make contact with this young chief who thinks I'm called

"Friend", although how in God's name I'll be able to coax him back into the governor's house is another matter altogether.'

'Don't go alone, Daniel!' Esther urged him, her hand on his wrist. 'At least take some armed men with you.'

'And scare them off?' Daniel countered. 'If we turn up with weapons, it'll be a sign that we expect to fight with them, when all I want is to talk.'

'You don't even speak their language,' George reminded him.

'And they don't speak ours,' Daniel added. 'That's what this whole business is about, remember.'

'Daniel,' George said in a level but serious tone as he put down his wine. 'You're seeking out this native as a favour for the governor, but also as part of your military duties?'

'Yes, I suppose so,' Daniel conceded.

'Well — and I hate to pull rank on you like this — I'm *ordering* you not to go out there without taking some men with you. They can hide their arms in the undergrowth if that makes you feel any better, but you can't expose your neck like that, just sitting there waiting to be attacked. For all you know, the chappie you're looking for won't even be there and the rest of them will have you for breakfast.'

'Daniel,' Esther added, 'you owe it to Martha and all your unborn children to do as George advises — sorry, *orders* — you to do.'

8

Three days later, Daniel sat on a rock in Botany Bay at high tide, the saltwater spray occasionally soaking him from head to foot as he watched his borrowed line bouncing up and down in the advancing and retreating waves. It was well past noon, to judge by the height of the sun and he was baking hot in the convict clothes he'd commandeered for the occasion. He was also well aware of several sullen dark faces peering through the bushes from behind him and occasionally he caught sight of the sharpened tip of a spear. His soldier's instinct for danger made his flesh tingle and all his training and common sense led him to expect the agony of a shaft between his shoulder blades at any moment. No wonder he was sweating, he told himself.

A man was suddenly standing alongside him without warning and Daniel started in surprise, before reminding himself that the native had been so skilful in his approach that he could have stabbed him in the back, had he wished to do so. The fact that Daniel was still alive reassured him that the man meant him no harm.

'Friend?' Daniel asked softly.

The man's face creased into a broad smile as he replied, 'Friend.'

Daniel pointed to himself with his free hand. 'Daniel.' When there was no reaction, he tried again. 'Daniel.'

The man was clearly struggling to get the word out. 'Dan-Woo.'

That would do for a start, Daniel decided, and he pointed back at the man with raised eyebrows, hoping he would follow suit.

'Bennelong,' the man announced.

That's got the preliminaries out of the way, Daniel told himself, then looked round as Bennelong stared back at the bushes that ringed the cove, waved his hand in the air and called out something that was unintelligible to Daniel.

A boy of perhaps thirteen years of age came running silently down the beach, carrying a spear. Bennelong said something to him in his own language and pointed at the water. The boy raised his spear and waded thigh deep into the breaking surf, looking down intently at the seabed beneath as each wave retreated. Then he launched the spear into the water with the aid of some sort of device in his hand and plunged into the waves after it. He pulled the spear back out of the water and impaled on its tip was a large fish in its death throes. The boy pointed the end of the spear towards Bennelong, who pulled the fish from it, walked up to Daniel, bowed slightly, handed him the fish and said, 'Dan-Woo.'

Daniel thanked him, looked down at the still writhing gift in his hand and said, 'Fish.'

'Fidge,' Bennelong replied as he bowed again.

Daniel smiled in gratitude and held out his hand for the spear, intending to learn from the boy how to catch fish in this manner. The boy backed off with a look of fear in his eyes and Bennelong said something to him. The boy ran back up the beach and came back a few moments later with some dry grass and a few twigs. Bennelong made a circle of beach stones, placed the grass and some of the twigs inside it, then began striking two stones together. In no time at all the collection of wood had become a small flame, onto which he placed more of the twigs. He held out his hand for the fish and when Daniel handed it back he rubbed the scales off it with one of the sharp stones, then placed it on top of the rocks in such a way that it could cook without becoming scorched.

Daniel pointed to the burning collection and said, 'Fire.'

'Fy-yer,' Bennelong repeated.

Daniel held out his hand and Bennelong grasped it eagerly, then pointed to the ground and sat down. Daniel followed suit and while they waited for the fish to cook, they began to exchange names for things like 'sun', 'sand', 'hand' and 'sea'. When the fish was ready, Bennelong took another sharp stone, placed the fish on a flat rock, cut it in half and handed half of it to Daniel, while retaining the other half. Daniel cried out in pain as the fish in his hand began to burn him and his portion dropped into the sand. Bennelong laughed pleasantly, got up, walked a few feet away and returned with a small piece of tree branch. He cut his remaining portion of fish into two pieces, impaled one half of it onto the end of the stick and handed it to Daniel, who said 'thank you' as clearly as he could and began to eat. The fish was only half cooked, but it was a small price to pay for the progress so far.

Then came the trickiest part of the whole operation. Bennelong had glanced once or twice in curiosity at the small rowing boat that Daniel had pulled up above the water line when he had arrived some hours earlier. When they finished eating, Daniel got up and walked to the water's edge next to the boat and bent down to wash his hands in the incoming surf. Bennelong had walked down with him and was gazing into the gunnels of the small craft.

'Boat,' Daniel said and waved his hand in a gesture for Bennelong to climb aboard. He did so and Daniel pushed the boat out, climbed in after him, unsheathed the oars and began to row through the surf out into the bay. A look of alarm spread across Bennelong's face, but Daniel reassured him by murmuring 'Friend' several times and was relieved when his passenger stood up with ease in the bottom of the bouncing craft and yelled something towards the disappearing shore. Reassuring himself that this was not a command for a rescue attack, Daniel kept rowing and was delighted to see several forms disappearing back into the woodland that fringed the bay. Bennelong had presumably advised them that he was going on a pleasure trip and would be back soon.

As they rounded the promontory at the end of the bay, a white face appeared cautiously from behind a rock on the top and only Daniel was aware of Private Drummond waving to a colleague further along the headland. A short while later, as their tiny vessel rocked and swayed in the choppy water on its way north to Sydney Cove, they passed a freshly lit beacon fire on the top of the cliff, which was followed almost immediately by an acknowledging one on the South Head, which could be seen from the lookout point on the island in the inner harbour they had named 'Rock Island'. It was the signal to the colony that Daniel had met with success and the governor would be waiting to welcome them ashore.

A large ship's cutter came into sight from the Cove entrance, rowed by six sailors in full uniform and Daniel stopped rowing. Their tiny vessel rocked from side to side and Bennelong looked nervously past Daniel's shoulder as he became aware of the oncoming naval contingent. Softly muttering 'Friend' repeatedly, Daniel kept smiling as he shipped the oars, leapt across into the cutter as it came alongside, then turned back with an outstretched hand, inviting Bennelong to do the same. Bennelong looked suspiciously, first at the sailors, then at the bottom of the cutter. Satisfied that they had no hidden weapons, he took the proffered hand and leapt into the larger boat. While one of the sailors tied Daniel's original dinghy to the back of the cutter, Daniel breathed a silent prayer of thanks that he had been allowed to do things his way.

The reception committee was waiting on the wharf as the cutter ground up against the wall and Daniel alighted first, holding out a hand for Bennelong to follow him. As they reached the top of the wharf, Daniel took Bennelong's hand and led him straight towards the governor, who stood, smiling, in his ceremonial uniform in the heat of the setting afternoon sun. Daniel pointed to the governor, said 'Friend', then walked up to Phillip and bowed, looking back at Bennelong with the word 'Chief'.

To everyone's amazement, Bennelong walked towards the governor, prostrated himself onto the ground, face down, repeating 'Chief', over and over again. The Reverend Johnson began to loudly intone a prayer that sounded more like an excommunication ceremony and Phillip had the presence of mind to raise Bennelong from the ground and repeat what he had heard Daniel say earlier.

'Friend.'

Bennelong smiled widely, then pointed back at Daniel. 'Friend. Dan-Woo.'

'You'd better come with us, Lieutenant,' Governor Phillip instructed him. 'Among other things, I have to give you Miss Mallett's ticket of leave, which I signed this morning, in anticipation of this happy outcome. I'm told she's somewhere in the crowd behind me, if you'd like to take a moment to be reunited with her.'

Daniel looked through the crowd with eager anticipation, but saw only Martha's back as she hurried up the slope from the wharf to the hut in which she was employed.

The proceedings that followed in Governor Phillip's house were both encouraging and comic. When offered food in the form of a dish of lamb, Bennelong grabbed it with both hands and tore at its flesh with perfect white teeth, before wiping his hands on his chest. When offered wine, he took one mouthful and spat it out with a torrent of words that were perhaps best left untranslated and when shown to the guest bedroom later that evening, he lay down on the floor and appeared to fall asleep instantly. Governor Phillip had asked Daniel to remain and gestured to an armchair in front of an empty fireplace, by a table on which sat a brandy decanter and two glasses. Governor Phillip took the other chair, poured two glasses, handed one to Daniel and raised his in a toast.

'What you have achieved today may well save the colony,' he beamed at Daniel. 'I have already kept my half of the bargain and I have great pleasure in handing you this official document which makes Miss Mallett the first to receive a ticket of leave on my watch. I also have some other news which you may find pleasing.'

Daniel remained silent as Phillip smiled.

'I have ordered Major Ross to transfer to Norfolk Island on a permanent basis, as governor of a second colony. Not only will it relieve some of the pressure on our resources, since there is every sign that Norfolk Island can be self-sufficient, but it also removes from our immediate company the man who tried to have you shot.'

'Who will be our new commanding officer?' Daniel asked, hoping that it would be George.

'That remains to be seen, after the anticipated Second Fleet finally gets here. It will bring its own consignment of marines and other officers from whom I may select. But I hope you approve of the transfer of Major Ross.'

'It's not really my place to comment, Governor,' Daniel replied modestly and tactfully, 'but there *is* one other favour I would ask.'

'Ask away,' Governor Phillip said.

'Could you consult your records and tell me when Miss Mallett's birthday is?'

9

'So I wonder who our new commander will be,' George commented as they stood surveying the ranks on morning parade, ahead of being marched in formation down to the wharf in order to welcome the officers and crew of the *Lady Juliana*, which lay at anchor in the Cove. 'He can't be any worse than the last one anyway.'

'Is it true that we're going to get a new governor as well?' Daniel asked.

'You'd have to hope not, since you've done so well out of the first one,' George grinned, 'but I did hear him tell Captain Tait that he's had enough of this place, which is proving hazardous to his health, apparently. Perhaps as a special favour, Captain Edgar will take him back to England when the *Lady Juliana* heads back.'

'Talking of favours, George, could I ask if you'd be prepared to hold a small party for Martha's birthday?'

'Shouldn't be a problem,' George assured him. 'Esther loves any form of social event. When is it?'

'August 9th.'

'Well, that gives us plenty of time to organise things. What did you have in mind?'

'Nothing really pretentious. Just a few people, some wine if we can wangle it, some more of your delicious fish and a speech from you welcoming her into our midst as a free woman, perhaps.'

'Talking of which,' George said, 'did you say something to upset her when you came back ashore with Bennelong?'

'Never even got to speak to her, why?'

'Just that she was in floods of tears and Esther wasn't sure if they were tears of relief to see that you'd got back safely, or if you'd managed to upset her again.'

'I don't set out to upset her, George — it just works out that way. Everything I say or do seems to go down the wrong way, so I've more or less given up. She seemed to be interested in that man Perkin, anyway.'

'Oh, that was just a ruse to get your attention,' George replied to Daniel's relief. 'She hasn't seen him for weeks. I gave her the ticket of leave certificate but she just looked at it, then stuffed it in her pocket like it meant nothing to her. Eyes front, here they come.'

A single cutter had pulled away from the *Lady Juliana* and was being rowed towards the wharf. George and Daniel marched their men down to the foreshore and stood at the entrance to the wharf, at attention. Daniel peered hard, but was unable to make out any military uniforms among the handful of men in the cutter, who all seemed to be civilians. Eventually the boat was moored to the iron ring set into the jetty wall and three civilians climbed unsteadily up the rope ladder slung from its side, clearly seeking to be reunited with their land legs. The marines presented arms as a mark of welcome and respect and George and Daniel walked towards the new arrivals, three men who looked ragged, under-nourished and grey in the face.

'Captain Johnston and First Lieutenant Bradbury, New South Wales Marine Corps. Welcome to Port Jackson.'

'Never mind all that,' the man in the centre of the new arrivals muttered. 'How many surgeons have you got?'

'Three altogether — why?' George asked, somewhat taken aback.

'Because, Captain,' the man replied, 'we're about to unload over two hundred women convicts and half of them are near dead from the voyage.'

'Two hundred, on a vessel *that* size?' Daniel couldn't help himself asking. 'We had one hundred on a larger vessel than that and even then it was a bit overcrowded.'

'You can thank your precious Admiralty for that,' the man snarled, then spat on the ground. 'I'm Thomas Edgar and it's been my miserable duty to steer that rotting hulk with its pestilential cargo for over three hundred days of sheer hell. This man is my ship's surgeon, name of Halliday, and he's half dead with fatigue and despair. We'll need tents on the beach to lay out the dying, hospitals for the ones we can save and deep holes for the ones who're already dead. We heaved two over the side out by that headland on the way in, but I gather that two more have died while we've been at anchor. It's not cholera — more likely simple starvation.'

'Where's the rest of your fleet?' George asked.

'God knows,' Edgar replied. 'We last saw the *Neptune* as we left the Cape and she was limping in. She and the *Surprize* and the *Scarborough* have the male convicts and we assume that they're somewhere behind us. We did have a fifth one, the *Guardian*, but she broke up near the Cape on her way in and the convicts who weren't drowned were due to be transferred to the *Neptune*, which no doubt only served to overcrowd it even more. There's a supply ship, the *Justinian*, somewhere behind us, but she's faster than the rest, so should get here soon.'

'Do you have any marines?' George asked.

'They're spread among the male convict vessels,' Edgar told him. 'They're under the command of a Captain Paterson on board the *Gorgon*, but their real commanding officer's still back in London, waiting for the next fleet, no doubt. I gather that Paterson has despatches for the governor.'

'The governor's waiting in his mansion to formally welcome you,' George said in a tone of voice that lacked real enthusiasm. 'I'm his adjutant, by the way.'

'So you have his authority?' Edgar asked.

'Of course.'

'Well, in that case, give his Excellency my apologies and tell him that I'm too busy unloading my ghost ship. Perhaps your men could be ordered to help with that.'

Daniel was sent to round up as many surgeons as he could locate, plus convict women who had been roughly trained in nursing as part of their sentences and he detailed a handful of marines to erect tents above the high-water mark. He took one look at the pathetic, stinking, half-starved and lice-ridden wrecks who had once no doubt been attractive women, but who were now being decanted unceremoniously onto the shingle as if they were bags of flour and sent also for the Reverend Johnson, who passed mournfully among the dead and dying with his prayer-book in his hand and a look of shock and revulsion on his face.

At sunrise the following morning, George sought out Daniel, and took him to see Governor Phillip.

'We're likely to be under attack in the near future,' Governor Phillip told them. 'It looks like the native fellows want their man back, which is a disaster, since we've just begun to get some sense out of him. But there's a whole tribe of them up at the south-west end, near the brickworks. I want you two to take a large detachment of men and show them that our friendship stretches only so far.'

'My family are up there!' George gasped. 'Permission to get back up there without delay, Governor?'

'Yes, of course. Take Bradbury here with you, since he seems to have a gift for getting through to them. And at least a dozen men, fully armed. We can't show them any sign of weakness.'

As they approached George's hut, Daniel could see Esther standing outside, wringing her hands in anguish and looking down towards them. George rushed over and hugged her gratefully and she asked, 'Is it true? Are the natives coming to revenge themselves for Daniel taking their chief? Martha's hiding in the back room with Roseanna and George Junior, but should we make a run for it down to the shore?'

'Just go inside with Martha and the children,' George instructed her, 'while we go and find out what's got the natives rattled. Daniel's good at talking to them, so don't worry.'

Daniel did his best to look confident as they carried on up the slope, past the edge of the forest and down the track to the brickworks. As they got to within a hundred yards of its entrance, a spear landed in the earth ahead of them and a tall native stepped out. The men halted on a command from George and as more natives appeared behind the first, the two groups stood eyeing each other in an uneasy silence.

The man who had presumably thrown the spear called out, 'Friend.'

'Over to you, Lieutenant Friend,' George muttered nervously.

Daniel stepped forward so as to be standing clear of the rest of the men. He pointed to his own chest. 'Me Friend. Daniel.'

There was an excited chatter among the natives and a young woman was pushed to the front.

The man in command of the tribal group pointed to the woman and shouted, 'Barangaroo. Bennelong.'

Daniel pointed back down the track they had just walked up, towards the main settlement. 'Bennelong. Friend.'

The man broke into what might have been a smile, but it was difficult to tell beneath all the scars that criss-crossed his face. He pointed in the same direction. 'Barangaroo. Friend Bennelong.'

'Far be it from me to teach you your business, old chap,' George muttered from the corner of his mouth, 'but I believe he wants you to take this lass down to Bennelong.'

Daniel pointed to the woman, then pointed back down the track.

Excited chatter broke out among the natives and the marines behind Daniel began nervously shouldering their muskets. George ordered them to ground them, offering a court martial to the first one to prime his powder and while he was doing so, the natives melted back into the bushes as fast as they had appeared in the first place, leaving the woman standing alone and looking fearful.

Daniel smiled and pointed to her. 'Barangaroo?'

'Barangaroo,' the woman confirmed.

Daniel pointed back down the track again. 'Bennelong?'

The woman said something in an excited response and Daniel held out an open hand in a gesture that she was to accompany him. The marines melted to the side and let the two of them through, then formed up behind them and accompanied them down the slope, Barangaroo a few feet from Daniel's side, looking from side to side with wide eyes as they began to pass the first outlying convict huts.

As they approached George's hut, George detached himself and ran in. Daniel heard several joyful shouts, then Esther and Martha appeared at the window, each with a child in their arms. As they passed the hut, Martha said quietly, but loudly enough for Daniel to hear, 'Did you buy *her* in exchange for a ticket of leave?'

As they approached Bennelong's hut, he raced out and embraced Barangaroo, before apparently ordering her into his hut. Then he turned back, embraced Daniel in a tight body hug and let fly a torrent of words in his own language, of which Daniel was only able to make out 'Dan-Woo' and 'Friend'.

10

As predicted, the next ship to arrive was the stores vessel *Justinian* and her cargo was eagerly unloaded by teams of convicts under military guard. Two weeks after that, the first of the male convict ships began limping into the Cove and dropping anchor and within two days they had run out of tents to house the half-dead victims of what, upon investigation, turned out to be a massive fraud by the owners of the chartered vessels, who had been paid for the number of convicts they had taken on board, whether they arrived alive or dead. It was necessary to open a new graveyard and Reverend Johnson no longer needed to carry his prayer-book to funerals, since he knew the words off by heart. However, he steadfastly refused to preside over mass burials, which earned him the grudging respect of the convicts who had been in Port Jackson for some time and could well appreciate what the dead must have suffered. A decent, respectful, Christian burial was the least that they could be afforded.

In mid-July, as George snapped to attention to collect his daily orders from the weary-looking governor, Phillip invited him to take a seat. He called for a pot of tea and offered a cup to George before sinking back in his padded chair and sighing.

'We're in deep shit, Captain.' When George didn't reply, the governor clearly felt the need to unburden himself more fully. 'The Second Fleet brought us only dead bodies and more mouths we can't feed. I've already written a despatch to the Admiralty which hopefully will have certain treacherous shipping agents hanged for murder and that will be going back on the *Lady Juliana*, since she's under orders to return with all speed to collect another lot. I've also asked London to relieve me of my office.'

George's eyebrows shot up in surprise and Phillip smiled.

'You can hardly be surprised, Captain. Call me a rat leaving a sinking ship, if that analogy isn't too close to the quick to be amusing, but you must have realised for yourself that this experiment has failed. The *Justinian* didn't unload enough supplies to even feed the extra convicts that the Second Fleet delivered and we were already short. My health has taken a decided turn for the worse since we've been out here and I cannot in all honesty blame it on the climate. Defeat has a debilitating effect on a lifelong military man such as myself and if I stay here much longer I'll be joining those poor buggers in the new graveyard we've had to open.'

'I'll be sorry to see you go, sir,' was all that George could say. 'Could I ask if you'd recommend me as adjutant to the next governor?'

'You may not be here yourself, George,' Governor Phillip told him. 'The choice will be yours, of course, but that's the main thing I have to tell you this morning. Captain Paterson came ashore carrying orders to establish a new marine regiment out here, completely independent of the Corps we have at present. The thinking back in London is that your men were only ever required to guard the convicts on the way out here and provide an armed guard while we got established. You are all entitled to return on the vessels you see anchored in the Cove and be demobilised back in London.'

'What if we don't want to go, sir?'

'That will depend upon whether or not I'm replaced, since I imagine that any new governor will have his own ideas. But if it's left to me, a distinct regiment will be formed from those of you who wish to remain and I'd be a lot happier if you would assume command of it. But if you'd prefer to go back to London with your new family, I'll authorise their return passage as well. Clearly you'll need to think things over, but I want you to pass on to your men that they'll be free to leave in a month or so, should they wish. Any who choose to remain will obviously be drafted into your new regiment, should you also decide to stay.'

'As you say, sir, I need to think about it. And of course I'll need to consult Esther, but surely she can't leave the colony without a free pardon?'

'And do you think I *wouldn't* grant her one, after all your service to me?'

'That's very generous of you, sir, but we wouldn't want to abandon our loyal nursemaid to her fate.'

'That's Bradbury's woman, isn't it?'

'Yes, sir, except they seem to be going through rather a difficult phase in their relationship at present.'

'Well, I can't grant free pardons to every woman who's got herself a marine who wants to go back to London. That would obviously encourage the more promiscuous of them to throw themselves at a marine, just to get out of here. Although I wouldn't blame them.'

'No, sir.'

Governor Phillip sat thinking for a moment, then looked back at George. 'Talking of Bradbury, he seems to have a unique gift with the natives, does he not?'

'They certainly seem to trust him sir, why?'

'Are the natives still keeping watch on us from up near the brickworks?'

'Yes sir — there seem to be more of them every day.'

'And your hut's up that way, isn't it?'

'Yes, sir — I was going to ask you if we might move further down the hill, since you raise the matter. Esther and Martha are getting quite nervous.'

'But you have other marines up there, do you not?'

'Yes, sir, as it happens. The hut next to ours has five marines in it.'

'And what detail are *they* on?'

'Just lately they've been in charge of unloading parties from the new fleet.'

'Why don't you put them on brickworks detail? That way, they can guard you from over-curious natives as well.'

'I *did* think of that, sir, but they're only young and a bit hot-headed and I'd be scared that they'd provoke an incident.'

'Even with Bradbury in command of them?'

'I'm not sure I follow you, sir.'

'Bradbury huts down here somewhere, in the Rocks area, doesn't he? I'm suggesting that you reallocate him to the hut next to yours. That way, he'll be on hand if the natives get a bit uppity and your women can feel that bit more reassured of their safety. Plus, of course, Bradbury would be closer to his own woman. It might push them together more quickly.'

'You obviously haven't seen how they stalk around each other like circling dogs, sir,' George grinned back. 'But the idea's a splendid one and at the end of the day, Bradbury will have to obey orders.'

Daniel's brain was in a turmoil after George passed on the news. He could, if he wished, return to England, but *then* what? He'd left civilian life in the first place in order to run away from a broken heart and he had no wish to do so again; nor did he wish to continue in the marines, to be sent anywhere in the world on board some leaky vessel that was under-supplied and probably barely seaworthy. And he couldn't bear the thought of not seeing Martha ever again.

But why should he stay, just for Martha? To see her daily — as he was more or less condemned to do, now that George had ordered him to move into the hut next to his — was the worst form of mental torture he could imagine. She studiously avoided looking across at him if she was outside with the children and she had curtly cut short every attempt he had made to engage her in conversation. He dearly longed to make her his wife, but the time for doing that was surely long past. He should have done it when she was so blatantly offering herself to him, or was that yet another of her clever performances?

Certainly, it had now become more complicated. It was bad enough that she had been repelled by the idea that he had somehow bought her by obtaining her ticket of leave in return for bringing in Bennelong and nothing would persuade her that he would have done so anyway and that the governor had simply added that into the mix *after* he'd agreed. What would she say now, if he proposed marriage to her and she knew that by accepting she was being offered a chance to return to London with a free pardon? If a ticket of leave was like buying a prize heifer at market, what did that make a free pardon and a return to London? And if they went back there, would she resume her former life and bring shame upon him by getting herself jailed?

He was turning those gloomy thoughts over and over in his head when Barangaroo stepped out of the hut she shared with Bennelong and stood before him, smiling in an embarrassed way. She had something in her hand and held it out towards him. Daniel took it from her and began to admire it and she slipped quickly back into the hut, clearly determined that what she had just handed him was a gift of some sort.

Daniel marvelled at the painstaking work that must have gone into it. It was a long necklace of some sort, made from a strong string that she must have acquired from the rubbish piled permanently at the side of the Commissary Store. Into it she had threaded a dozen or more pieces of patiently polished ornamental driftwood that she must have collected from the shoreline and had interspersed them with tiny shells from the same source. It was a totally unique piece of native craft and at least Daniel had solved another problem. He now knew what to give Martha for her birthday.

11

August 9th dawned and Daniel's heart was already in his mouth when he awoke and realised that it was 'the day'. He had a present for Martha's birthday and an invitation to the select party that George was organising. Surely she couldn't help but be pleased and perhaps engage in a longer conversation in which Daniel could plead with her to put him out of his indecision. He had made up his mind that if she spurned him once more, he'd return to England, leave the marines and find some sort of commercial position in the City, where his early grounding in the commerce of import and export in his native Bristol might earn him a desk in a dreary dockside warehouse. If she just gave him *some* indication, however slight, that they might have a future, then he would remain and join the regiment that George was excitedly talking about all the time. Clearly, they were all remaining and Esther must have foresworn the opportunity of a free pardon in order to remain with George here in the colony, giving him both things that his heart most craved. If only Martha would do the same for him, he would make her the Queen of New South Wales, if that's what she wanted.

The smell of fish drifted across on the evening air as Daniel walked slowly across the narrow grass division between the huts, feeling like a prisoner being led to the gallows, clutching in his hand the necklace that Barangaroo had given him, wrapped in a piece of gun cloth.

'Come on in, Daniel,' Esther enthused as he stepped into the hut. She raised her voice and called towards the back room, 'Martha, here's Daniel, and by the look of things he has a present for you.'

Martha came through and Daniel held the present out. Martha took it from him with a downcast look and opened up the cloth. She gave a slight gasp and a grin of delight flickered across her face before she regained her self-control and looked back up at Daniel with a cold stare. 'I don't want a gift made by your whore.'

Daniel choked and turned away, as if hit by a musket ball. He stumbled blindly back out through the front door and raced back to his own hut.

Later that evening, Daniel was lying in bed when he heard the sound of someone creeping into his hut. Quickly grabbing his bayonet he stealthily crept forward and was stunned when he walked straight into Martha. They stared hard at each other in the torchlight above Martha's head, then both burst out laughing.

'Come and sit on the front step,' Martha invited him. 'We don't want your men to get the wrong idea and I need to apologise to you. Esther explained to me that you are not in a relationship with the native woman, and that it was your idea to plan me a birthday party.'

'The men won't be back until dawn,' Daniel told her, 'but we do need to talk.'

There was an awkward silence as they sat, thighs touching, on the narrow front step under the stars of a clear sky. Eventually it was Daniel who spoke. 'Can we start again?'

'What, put me back below decks?' Martha joked.

'Not quite, but I think we may have got on the wrong side of each other. I realise that you were insulted by the suggestion that I had in some way ... well, *compromised* you by getting you that ticket of leave. It was the governor's sole idea, I swear, and he didn't come up with it until I'd already agreed to bring Bennelong in.'

'Bennelong?'

'That native who seems to regard me as his friend. The woman who made your necklace is his wife.'

'You were very brave, bringing him in like that, exposing yourself to slaughter. We were all very relieved to see you come back in one piece.'

Daniel reached out and took her hand. 'How did you feel when you thought I might not come back?'

'Like someone was ripping my heart out,' Martha admitted as she squeezed his hand.

Daniel's voice began to crack with emotion. 'You've no idea what it means to me to hear you say that. I've never felt this way about a woman in my entire life, I swear. I just can't imagine staying out here and only seeing you from time to time and the two of us chatting politely like bored vicars at a church conference. What I'm trying to say is ... well...'

'You want to marry me?'

'Yes.'

'Well why didn't you say so *months* ago?'

'I was going to, that night you were dancing with Private Perkin, but I never got the chance.'

'And I only danced with him to get you jealous. What a stupid pair we are.'

'So will you marry me?'

'Only if you assure me that I'm not being acquired like a piece of property.'

'Wait there a moment.' Daniel disappeared back inside the hut and reappeared with a small soft felt bag and handed it to her. 'This was my mother's and it probably doesn't fit, but it's all I have. Martha, will you marry me?'

'Oh yes — yes!' Martha squeaked as she threw her arms around him and smothered his face in kisses.

Daniel and Martha were married only three months later, and Martha quickly fell pregnant. Once she discovered that Martha was with child, Esther insisted on recruiting another nursemaid for her own children. George also took it upon himself to restrict Daniel to the single, but important, command of the men guarding the brickworks.

It was an important duty for several reasons. The first was the urgent need for bricks. The colony had long since abandoned the laborious policy of building in stone blocks, with the result that the Governor's House and the Commissary Store would stand out uniquely in Port Jackson's architecture for many years to come. The mud of the Tank Stream had proved to be eminently suitable for the baking of bricks and tiles, with which most of the house-builders among the convict class were more familiar anyway and the Barracks had risen rapidly as kiln after kiln discharged thousands and thousands of their distinctive dark brown product that was carted daily half a mile downhill and was now being converted into a half-decent hospital.

The second reason was because the brickworks had become a recognised meeting point between the settlers and the natives. Bennelong had slipped away from his hut, taking Barangaroo with him, many weeks previously. He had never officially been a prisoner, but the permanent presence of armed guards outside his hut 'for his own protection' had been a diplomatic pretence that fooled no one, least of all those being 'protected' and the two natives had demonstrated their contempt for their white gaolers by slipping away totally undetected at dead of night. But two weeks later, Bennelong had returned, with no obvious trace of embarrassment or apprehension and had demanded that the governor supply him with a hut of his own choosing, at a location that seemed to be of some ceremonial or religious significance to him on Lookout Point, which soon became more generally known as 'Bennelong Point'.

But he had also set a precedent and had no doubt reported back to members of his tribe that the settlers — and particular the tribal chief they called 'Governor' — could be prevailed upon to provide goods and other benefits in exchange for their company and a few simple pieces of advice on what to catch for food, how to catch it and how best to plant seeds in the ground in such a way as to encourage them to grow. The result was the almost daily arrival, at the brickworks, of groups of eager natives who wished to be escorted down to Bennelong's hut. There was an ever-present risk that young hotheads among the marines might misinterpret their arrival so George had experienced no difficulty in explaining to the governor why it was important to have Daniel on hand, to act as host, guide, interpreter and mediator.

Early one autumn evening, as Daniel and Martha sat on the front step of their two-roomed love palace, holding hands and thinking up children's names, George shouted across from next door, 'Bring your table and chairs out into the fresh air and prepare to taste the most amazing seafood you ever experienced.'

A few minutes later he and Esther appeared from next door, smilingly carrying a plate of what looked like red cornets and a jug of Esther's home-made wine. They sat eagerly round the table as Daniel poured the wine and George enthused about his latest acquisition.

'Some of my men went up to Broken Bay, to escort the governor up the river he's named Hawkesbury, apparently as part of his policy of expanding the colony. While they were staying overnight, they came across a bunch of natives fishing for these things in the rocks, then dropping them in boiling water and eating them. One of them offered some to Private Gooding and they turned out to be delicious, so the marines spent a whole day fishing for several bagsful, much to the governor's annoyance until he tried one himself. A bit like the oysters you can get in expensive London restaurants, although you have to mess around pulling off their shells in order to eat the flesh inside. Try one.'

'What are they called?' Martha asked.

'No idea,' George replied. 'The natives have a name for them, but like every name they give things, you'd sprain your tongue trying to repeat it. I call them "fish crescents". What do you think?'

The appreciative murmurs eliminated any doubt as to whether or not a new ocean treat had been discovered and Martha immediately ordered a bagful for herself and Daniel, should Private Gooding venture north again. Then George's face assumed a serious look. 'Actually, this isn't just a social visit. We all have to make some important decisions within the next month or so. I promised the governor I'd sound out your opinions, but we both hope that you'll go along with what Esther and I have decided.'

'We're finally being disbanded?' Daniel guessed.

'I'm afraid so,' George confirmed. 'That new chap who came out on the *Gorgon* — Captain Paterson — has already taken over the Barracks with that bunch of marines that came out with him. They're the spearhead of a new lot to replace us and he came out with a commission as Lieutenant-Governor. Apparently there's someone higher ranked than him coming over in the next lot and in the meantime the governor's sending Paterson and his mob over to Norfolk Island. That leaves me in temporary command until the new man comes out, but since we're being disbanded anyway, there's no promotion in it for me.'

Daniel chuckled. 'I'd love to see Ross's face when Paterson lands over there and strips him of his command.'

'Apparently Ross's coming back here briefly, before sailing for England when the *Neptune* raises anchor. The governor would like to depart with him, but he's stuck here until he gets a despatch relieving him of command. In the meantime he's trying to pretend he still runs the colony and will no doubt be very relieved to see the back of Paterson. But the writing's on the wall for the New South Wales Marine Corps, I'm afraid.'

Martha seized Daniel's arm and looked apprehensive. 'What's going to happen to us all? We can't go back, even as service wives, until we've served our terms and Esther and I still have at least another three years out here. Will we have to fend for ourselves?'

'Not necessarily,' George reassured her. 'That's what we need to talk about. The governor asked me to form a new regiment, but apparently Paterson put the dampers on that and insists that any force of armed soldiers must come under the overall command of this chap who's still in London.'

'What's his name?' Daniel asked.

'Grose, apparently. I don't know what rank he is, but presumably it's higher than Captain. Anyway, the governor sat down with this Paterson chap and struck a deal. The bottom line is that I'll be forming a separate company recruited from men of our lot who don't want to go home on the *Neptune* and I imagine that will include you, Daniel.'

'Of *course* it will,' Martha insisted. 'I'm sure Daniel wouldn't want to go home without me, leaving me here to fend for myself and with a baby on the way.'

'If anyone could survive in those circumstances, living by their wits, *you* could,' Daniel added, pecking Martha on the cheek, 'but Martha speaks for both of us. Our child will be born here in the colony and I'll be here to look after them both, so count me in for the new company, George. I assume I'll keep my rank?'

George grinned. 'Somehow, I thought that would be your answer. But I haven't told you the whole story yet.'

'Go on,' Daniel and Martha said, almost in unison.

'Well, as you can imagine, the governor's pretty miffed that he's obliged to remain here under the diplomatic equivalent of house arrest, with Grose calling the shots from London, so he wants to move out west, to where you took him a couple of years ago, Daniel.'

'Rose Hill?'

'That's the place. He's ordered a house to be built on what he calls "The Crescent". It seems that James Ruse has managed to grow wheat out there and the governor's convinced that the whole area could become a permanent food supply for the colony, so he wants to set up an experimental farm out there, with Ruse as its manager and this new company of mine guarding it.'

'What do *we* know about farming?' Daniel pointed out.

'I know a bit, about dairy farming anyway,' George replied. 'I ran my parents' food lot business back home and I used to visit dairy farms around the area. I picked up quite a few useful things about cows in the process, like never to stand behind one while it's being milked. But we wouldn't be going out there as farmers, anyway. The governor, quite sensibly, is of the opinion that once we start successfully producing food, the natives will be raiding us on a nightly basis. In fact, to judge by Bennelong's antics, they could probably do it in broad daylight, right under our noses. As a result, the farm will need guarding round the clock. There's a barracks out there already as you know, Daniel, since you helped to set it up and the suggestion is that we form a separate company of this New South Wales Corps notionally under Grose, but out west and effectively independent, although he somehow expects me to supervise the deployment of men here in my spare time, at least until Grose arrives.'

'What's it like out there in the west?' Martha asked Daniel anxiously.

Daniel shrugged. 'Pretty wild when I was out there, but the governor may be right about it being good for growing food. There's fresh water flowing through a wide valley, before it empties into the tidal creek at a point which is a good day's march inland from here. The only natives we saw were hiding in the bushes as usual, but as George says they'll soon become more visible when we grow grain, and even more aggressive if we begin keeping livestock that they can spear. But I wouldn't want to go out until Martha's had the baby. God knows the hospital here's pretty primitive, but there's *nothing* out there.'

'Martha won't be the first woman to give birth out here,' Esther said, having sat silently through the conversation thus far. 'I got a nurse of sorts when I gave birth to George Junior and this new woman I've got — Sarah — seems pretty good with children, although not as good as you were, Martha,' she added as she leaned across the table and placed a reassuring hand on Martha's arm. 'I'll ask Sarah what she knows about midwifery and if she manages to convince me, we'll take her with us.'

12

During the next few months several more vessels arrived from London and Cork, bringing more marines for Captain Paterson to install in the over-full barracks before he left for Norfolk Island and for George to notionally supervise once Paterson set sail. George had compiled a list of those men who were to form his company and they were drilled daily in the area immediately below where his hut and Daniel's were located. There were two good reasons for this.

First of all, detailed plans were being drawn up for the move up-river to Rose Hill and George wanted his men to remain drilled. Secondly, there had been friction between George and Captain Paterson, resulting from George's conscription of large numbers of convicts with skills he could use. Many of his labourers had found themselves undergoing boat training and had learned to heave an oar in the commandeered ships' cutters that could be used to transport men and materials a dozen or so miles upstream from the harbour to the jetty on the river from which Rose Hill could be reached following a further short march inland. It would take many journeys to establish the sort of developed settlement that Governor Phillip envisaged and since these journeys were regulated by the state of the tide, in order to make the rowing that much easier, they needed careful planning.

There had always been a weekly supply expedition, with the result that there were boatmen who knew the channel well and one day in late November, before the weather became too hot, George and Daniel jumped on board the cutter commanded by William Booth, a former Sussex fisherman. Booth stood in the stern with the rudder firmly in his hand as six muscular and bronzed convicts pulled the boat firmly away from the harbour jetty and headed across the bay and into the wide estuary that marked the sea exit of the river they were to follow upstream for several hours.

The river up which the incoming tide was driving them almost effortlessly became slowly narrower, and after an hour or so the man in the bow of their naval cutter stood up and began calling out the estimated depths to the helmsman and indicating with his arms whether to steer right or left. The overhanging vegetation crept right down to water level and occasionally they would spot a snake sliding through the undergrowth down to the water's edge, or an unfamiliar-looking creature crashing through the undergrowth as it was startled by their stealthy approach. The channel got narrower and narrower, until they rounded a bend and ahead of them on the left was a crudely constructed landing jetty, on which stood an officer and four men in full uniform.

The boat pulled up alongside the jetty and a uniformed private was detailed to take the rope thrown to him by the bowman and secure it to a bollard that had been driven into the ground at the side. Daniel stood aside to let George out first and there was the customary exchange of salutes and handshakes before George turned to Daniel.

'You presumably remember Lieutenant Bradbury, since he was the man who abandoned you here with your detachment. Daniel, this is Lieutenant John Macarthur,' George said as Daniel and Macarthur shook hands.

'I forgave him some time ago,' Macarthur replied in an accent that betrayed him as one born a West Countryman. 'If you don't mind a bit of a hike, I'll show you around and then we'll have dinner at the barracks.'

They strode up a slight slope along a well-beaten track, to a point at which water was cascading off a natural waterfall into the river up which they had just travelled.

'As you can see, gentlemen,' Macarthur pointed out, 'the sea water is only just below the lip of this natural weir, although at low tide the drop's about five feet. Upstream is fresh water and downstream is the salt stuff you just rowed through. If you'd care to follow me further up this rise, you can see how we put the fresh water to good use.'

As they reached the top of the rise, a natural valley opened up before them, halfway down which they could see a modest sized hill, on top of which was the crudely constructed palisade of the barracks and fort.

Macarthur waved his hand ahead of them. 'That's Rose Hill Barracks, obviously. Down below the fort, on the river bank, you can see a paddock of wheat grown by my fellow countryman Jim Ruse. He'll be joining us for dinner. We have a watermill and Jim grinds his own produce to give us our daily bread. Tastes like sawdust and breaks your teeth after a couple of days, but the governor wants to give Jim more land to cultivate. As you can see, there's plenty of land to spare and when I finish my term I'm hoping the governor can be persuaded to give me some of it. The grass out there looks suitable for sheep and I learned how to farm those in Devon, in between commissions. There's probably an inexhaustible market for mutton out here, once the colonists get tired of eating kangaroo.'

'Kangaroo?' George asked.

'Those bouncy animals you can see bounding around the place on their hind legs. The meat's very tough and although I've never actually eaten horse, I imagine that the experience would not be dissimilar. Kangaroo is the native name for them.'

'The governor's very keen on maintaining good relationships with the locals,' Daniel told him.

Macarthur snorted. 'He probably won't be if he comes to live out here. That's where we're building his house, by the way,' he indicated with a wave of the hand towards the elevated ground. 'Thought we'd better keep it within the compound, unless he wants spears whistling through his dining room.'

Daniel narrowed his gaze and could make out a large construction inside the barracks compound that appeared to be about six courses high in bricks.

'When do you think it'll be ready?' George asked.

'Sometime early next year, with a bit of luck. I'm hoping to impress the old misery, so that when my term ends I might persuade him to grant me some land in exchange for my discharge pension.'

'You're not signing up for another term in George's new company?' Daniel asked.

'No,' Macarthur replied. 'I could stay out here forever as a soldier, but my wife Elizabeth has other ideas and she reckons that our two sons would enjoy better prospects out here as farmers rather than as soldiers. Anyway, we'll have to wait and see how things work out. How are things going with Paterson back there?'

'He thought he ran the colony,' George said, 'and in reality he probably did, which is why the governor booted him across the water. I was hoping you'd transfer to my company at level rank when we make the final break, although we'll still be under the notional command of Paterson and above him that chap Grose who's still stalking around London.'

'What's Grose like — have you met him?' Daniel asked.

Macarthur shook his head. 'Never met him, but rumour has it that he leaves everything to his seconds in command. So it looks as if Paterson's the one to keep well in with, when he's not picking wild flowers.'

'A figure of speech?' Daniel asked, amused by the mental picture of a senior military officer picking flowers.

'Far from it,' Macarthur asserted. 'That's how he got his position out here, apparently, by promising to send specimens back to Sir Joseph Banks, one of those armchair jokers in London who dreamed up this whole idea of a colony of New South Wales.'

'Remind me to send him a posy of them when we get back,' George chuckled. 'Now tell me how you're getting on with the natives.'

Macarthur frowned. 'They're a funny lot. They sit out by the river most days, fishing with spears. Occasionally we can hear them singing and dancing quite harmlessly and they even built a couple of huts in clear view of us. From all that, you'd conclude that they want to co-exist in peace with us, but any man going out of the fort alone, or unarmed, is likely not to come back, and they steal any piece of equipment we're unwise enough not to bring back inside.'

'You heard that we managed to befriend a few of them and even began to converse with them?' Daniel asked.

'Good luck to you with that,' Macarthur said. 'We'll leave things as they are out here, if it's all the same to you, Lieutenant. We stay on our side of the fence and they stay on theirs. Talking of fences, here we are. Dinner's in the main mess hall in an hour or so.'

After washing his hands and face to get the dust off them before eating, Daniel wandered out of the front door, where

George stood smoking his pipe and contemplating the landscape.

'Penny for your thoughts?' Daniel offered.

'Just looking out there, at all that open land,' George said. 'The governor's talking about expanding the experimental farm and I was wondering if there'd be any land left for Macarthur — or maybe even me.'

Daniel shot him a surprised look. 'You thinking of resigning your commission, after persuading me to stay on?'

'I just don't like the way matters are heading, that's all,' George replied. 'By the sound of it, this Grose fellow in London will just leave Paterson in charge and he and I will never see eye to eye.'

'If you go, I might go with you,' Daniel said. 'You've always looked after me and if you and Paterson part on bad terms, he'll have me marked down as one of the enemy.'

'It's a pity that all these politics had to come out here with us, isn't it?' George said as he struck the bowl of his pipe against his boot in order to tip out the spent tobacco. 'When I signed up to come out here, I thought it would be a brand new start for everybody. No stupid officers, no old enmities, no climbing on other people's corpses to get to the top.'

'I'm not sure what I expected when I came out,' Daniel replied. 'Not that I had much choice. But I certainly didn't expect to finish up with a wife and child.'

'Me neither,' George agreed. 'But the big question is — what do we do if we resign our commissions?'

'Plenty of land out there,' Daniel answered with a nod towards the miles and miles of open scrub with the occasional patch of forest. 'Fancy farming?'

'Not really. Right now, though, I fancy some dinner. Let's go in.'

'What's it like for a woman living out here?' Daniel asked Elizabeth Macarthur. She raised her eyebrows over her soup bowl and Daniel hastened to explain his reason for enquiring. 'Pardon my curiosity, but I'm recently married and my wife's expecting a baby next May.'

'How nice!' Elizabeth replied. 'If I deduce correctly, your real question is what are the chances of a woman safely delivering in this wilderness?'

'Something like that,' Daniel conceded.

'I gave birth to our first son in an army hospital in Gibraltar, under the tender mercies of a so-called military surgeon who I can only assume was trained in veterinary science,' Elizabeth replied. 'Out here my second son was born in a tent in Port Jackson, but the woman who delivered him was a midwife, so was able to tell which end came first. If you possibly can, have your wife taken back down to Sydney when she's almost due, unless you're bringing your own midwife with you. I certainly strongly advise against leaving her to the butchers in our so-called barracks hospital, who only know how to stitch up what *can* be stitched and hack off what can't.'

It fell quiet for a moment, just as a convict servant entered the room with a tray full of plates, each of which he served in turn to the lunch guests from the tray he'd first placed on a side table. George looked down at the pie on his plate and sniffed suspiciously at the steam that was rising out of its crust.

'Eel pie,' Macarthur told him. 'Speciality of the house.'

As George plunged his knife into the crust to release the heat, Macarthur reverted to what seemed to be his favourite topic of conversation.

'Like everything, you soon get tired of the taste, even if it *is* to your liking. One day, if I get my way, everyone will be heartily sick of the taste of roast lamb, although right now I'd give a week's pay for a plate full of it.'

'Do you really think the land would support sheep?' George asked.

'Without a doubt. The only real risk would be that the natives would spear them all at night, before we got to culling them ourselves. We'd need to build a massive fence around the stock grazing land and post men with muskets at regular intervals.'

'As you probably know, the governor has in mind a vastly expanded experimental farm,' Jim Ruse chimed in, before puffing out his chest and adding, 'As a matter of fact, he's asked me to manage it for him, but I suppose I'll be working from behind a ten foot stockade.'

'Not necessarily,' Daniel told him. 'We managed to strike up a decent relationship with the natives in Sydney and I'm sure that if you somehow found a way of rewarding some of the locals out here for guarding your animals for you, they'd be safe enough.'

'Daniel has a way with the natives,' George explained. 'But I suspect that the lot out here are a different tribe altogether. What do the natives call this place? The governor shares Daniel's enthusiasm for peaceful co-existence and would deem it a bonus if he could at least get its name right.'

'You have a choice of two possibilities,' Macarthur told him. 'The natives on this side of the river call it "Paramada", while on the far side it seems to be called "Burramatta". It may be neither, of course, but we hear the words so often that I think they're place names. Either that or they are terms for "white bastards who stole our land."'

'John!' his wife protested.

'Sorry, dear — I spend too long with soldiers. But I was a soldier when you married me, so you knew what to expect.'

'And how long do you intend to carry on being a soldier?' George asked craftily, remembering their earlier conversation and in the belief that he might be more truthful in his wife's presence.

'Until he can get out decently and earn a proper living!' Elizabeth announced on his behalf.

Macarthur sighed. 'Elizabeth fails to appreciate that one cannot resign from the army as easily as one can from, for example, a post in a bank or a trading company. I've notionally got another year or so to go, but there's no reason why I can't begin to chase my dreams on a part-time basis. A sheep farm out there somewhere, with enough soldiers under my command to ensure that they're properly guarded.'

'I'll try to pretend I didn't hear that,' George joked, 'since you'll still be under my command even when these new arrangements come into force. But then you'll be the Commandant of Rose Hill Barracks as part of the Fourth Company of the New South Wales Corps, with this mystery man Grose as your ultimate commanding officer, William Paterson as his absentee dogsbody and the governor running a very poor third place.'

'Is it true that the governor's losing his grip on the colony?' Elizabeth asked. 'We hear rumours to that effect all the time, but we're so far away from where it's happening, stuck out here in the middle of "woop", as I call it. That's the noise the birds make out there,' she explained when Daniel burst out laughing.

'That was a wonderful imitation,' he congratulated her. 'You and my wife will get on handsomely. She's an actress and a talented mimic.'

'An actress?' Elizabeth echoed. 'How simply wonderful! I do so miss the theatre.'

'You may not be missing it for much longer,' Daniel told her. 'The governor wanted Martha — that's my wife — to open a theatre of some sort in Sydney, but there's no reason why she couldn't start here.'

'The main problem would be the lack of women,' Elizabeth replied wistfully. 'One or two of the men are married, and of course we have a few female convicts employed in menial tasks, but clearly convict women would be *quite* unsuitable for the theatre.'

13

Sarah Biddle, Esther's convict nursemaid, was able to make good her claim to midwifery skills twice in the middle months of 1792. First was the delivery of Matthew, Daniel and Martha's firstborn, on a hot sultry night in mid-May. Martha's screams and pleas for mercy woke everyone within a half-mile radius, as Daniel paced nervously up and down outside their hut, listening with foreboding and dread to what sounded like Martha's last few moments on earth, but consoled by Esther's regular trips outside from the back room in which the child was being delivered and in which she was periodically holding Martha's hand and mopping her brow.

'She didn't really mean that, you'll see,' Esther assured him as they heard Martha scream 'Never again!' for the fifth time. Then it went quiet and Daniel began mentally planning Martha's funeral until Esther hurried outside with a small, bawling bundle with a screwed up red face that reminded Daniel of one of the rats they had spotted on the river bank during their upstream journey to Rose Hill.

'There you go,' Esther enthused as she handed him the bundle. 'Congratulations, and before you ask, Martha's fine. She's asleep right now, but by sun-up you'll be able to go in and try to convince her that he's the most beautiful baby you've ever seen.'

'Thanks, Esther,' Daniel said. 'You really are such a wonderful friend to Martha and I and I'm sorry if we kept you up all night.'

'I'd never have been able to sleep through that racket anyway,' Esther assured him, 'and I bet if you were to go up the lines of huts on either side of us, you'd discover that everybody else is awake as well. But I wanted to see if Sarah really *was* fit to act as my midwife in a few weeks' time and I'm happy to report that she is. Unless you and George are thinking of joining a monastery, I think we'll retain her services for the meantime.'

In July, it was Esther's turn to do the screaming, Martha's choice to mop her brow and Sarah's second opportunity to demonstrate her skills. Robert Johnston was a healthy seven pounds in weight and a week later George insisted on 'wetting the baby's head' with some lethal concoction he'd brought back after a barracks inspection at Rose Hill two weeks previously and which generated a hangover that lasted them both for two days.

During Matthew's first few weeks of life, Martha adjusted to the unfamiliar but delightful sensation of having a helpless child at her breast and Daniel insisted on getting up during the night feeds in order to make tea on the woodstove that had been gratefully constructed by one of his convict brick workers whose trade had been in metalwork until transported for forgery of coins of the realm, and whom Daniel had opted not to report for turning up drunk for duty one day the previous September. George had taken one look at the bags under Daniel's eyes, declared him medically unfit for duty and given him two weeks' unofficial leave. Then he called in the favour when Governor Phillip decided to make one of his regular inspection tours of Rose Hill, taking with him, for his first visit to this increasingly important outpost, the recently arrived Lieutenant-Governor Francis Grose, who had dropped anchor in the *Pitt* on the same night that Martha had given birth.

'What's he like?' Daniel asked as they walked alongside each other down the slope to the harbour, keen to catch up on all the news and gossip following several intensive months up at the brick yards and several weeks on 'new father' duties.

'Seems affable enough,' George replied. 'Certainly a distinct improvement on Ross, who went back on the *Neptune*, along with rest of his deserters. He'd only been back from Norfolk Island a week when he picked a fight with one of Grose's lot and the governor used that as the final excuse to kick his arse and send him home.'

'There's an old saying about "Out of the frying pan into the fire",' Daniel reminded him. 'How do we know that Grose will be any better?'

'It's not Grose you need to worry about, it's Paterson, if he ever comes back from his exile on Norfolk Island. Grose looks every inch the lazy bastard Macarthur made him out to be, but you can form your own opinion — there he is, down on the wharf with the governor. We'd better step lively.'

The journey up river was uneventful, but some thirty minutes before they reached the landing jetty in the shallows where the sea met the fresh water, Daniel was surprised to see a much more substantial wharf on the south bank, jutting out into the deep water mid channel, which the helmsman of their cutter carefully skirted round. Governor Phillip waved over at it as he caught the look of surprise on Daniel's face.

'I'd forgotten that you haven't seen this before, Lieutenant,' he beamed. 'It was only finished last week and has yet to be christened, but it will take deep water craft direct from the Cove. That way we can get supplies directly up river without the need to store them temporarily in Sydney, where they can get pilfered.'

'I'd take a guess that the governor's planning to move his headquarters up here sooner than we thought,' George muttered under his breath to Daniel.

'And your guess would be correct,' came a voice from behind them and both men turned deep red when they realised that Lieutenant-Governor Grose had been listening in to their conversation. Grose nodded over the top of the river bank on their left-hand side and added, 'If you look carefully, I think you'll see the start of a straight road, intended to be several miles long, which will link the wharf with the new town. The governor asked me to find out the native name for the area, so that he can apply it to this new town he's so keen on. Any ideas?'

'Last time we were out here together,' George replied, 'Lieutenant Macarthur gave us a choice of two native names. One, so far as I recall, was "Paramada".'

'And the other was "Burramatta", to the best of my recollection,' Daniel added.

Grose thought for a moment. 'Let's combine the two, shall we?' He raised his voice to attract the attention of the governor, who was standing up in the bow of the boat, trying to get a better look over the bank at the convict working party that was building the new road he'd commissioned. 'Governor,' Grose shouted, 'we have a name for your new settlement — "Parramatta" — a combination of two local native names.'

'Excellent!' Governor Phillip beamed back. '"Parramatta" it shall be.'

As they breasted the short hill at the top of the well-worn path from the old landing jetty and past the river weir, then took in the valley below them, Daniel's eyebrows shot up in surprise at the development that had been taking place since his last visit there some months previously. There was a long straight road leading out from the barracks compound, down the rise and along the bank of the river, back in the direction from which they had come, which was clearly the other end of the road that was still under construction at the deep water wharf. On either side of the road men were already in the process of erecting daub and wattle convict huts of the type with which Sydney had begun its days, except that these had thatched roofs rather than those of the 'slab' variety.

In the barracks complex itself, the governor's house was all but completed and next to it was a stores building part-constructed from brick. A third building, upon which work seemed to have been temporarily halted, was no doubt intended as a hospital, and everywhere one looked within the compound there were signs of bustle and activity, with men carrying hods of bricks and lengths of timber, while others appeared to be mixing mortar in large piles, which other men were carrying in consignments to those who were laying bricks.

Below the compound, between the barracks and the river, was a large field that had been divided into three strips. In one could clearly be seen the stubble of last season's wheat crop and men turning it in by hand, using hoes to plough the rotting residue into the existing six inches of dark, fertile-looking soil. Next to it was half a field of yet to be harvested maize, suggesting that the first half had already been taken from the ground, while at the far end was a small hut, in front of which lay a cottage garden that from a distance appeared to be planted with cabbages, turnips and potatoes.

'That's the experimental farm,' Governor Phillip shouted back proudly over his shoulder. 'Ruse has done a wonderful job and all the land further upstream as far as that clump of trees has already been deforested ahead of the expansion that will begin once the weather cools. Then Macarthur has some scheme or other in mind, so I've given him a few acres beyond that to play around with.'

Daniel strained his eyes, but the line of trees partially blocked his view, although what was growing beyond them looked vaguely familiar from his voyaging days. He looked back closer to hand and his eyes lit upon a group of natives fishing in the river, with only a crude fence between the river bank and the boundary of the experimental farm. 'Presumably they have look-outs in the garrison, to prevent the natives making off with the crops, or attacking Ruse's cottage and all these huts along the road?' he asked George.

George looked slightly taken aback by the question and replied simply, 'We need to talk about that. Remind me on the return trip.'

There was a volley of fire from the walls of the palisade and a Union Jack rose into sight up the flagpole as the visiting party approached. Lieutenant Macarthur was waiting to welcome them, along with a detachment of his men and Daniel cheerfully shook his hand upon their being reacquainted. Then there was the predictably splendid three course dinner, with roast emu and locally grown root vegetables, washed down with cider made from locally coaxed sour apples. A lemon syllabub completed the handsome repast.

Daniel was curious. 'I'm no cook, but don't you need sugar for the syllabub?'

'Indeed you do,' Elizabeth Macarthur confirmed, 'and you can thank my husband for that.'

Suddenly Daniel remembered what was so familiar about the plants he had seen growing on the Macarthur allotment. 'You've planted sugar, haven't you?' He looked across the table at Macarthur. 'I remember those cane plants from my time in the West Indies.'

'I didn't have to plant them,' Macarthur told him. 'They were growing there naturally and I too spent time in the tropics, where they grow like weeds. The same with bananas, which I've discovered further down the valley. I learned enough in Barbados to be able to propagate more of both, so life out here will soon be much sweeter.'

'How are you going with the natives?' Grose asked.

'No trouble at all for the past six months or so. The only incidents were recorded in my log, but they were just minor acts of theft.'

'Bradbury here will be dealing with those once he moves out here, or so Captain Johnston tells me,' Governor Phillip announced.

Daniel dropped his dessert spoon and glared round at George, who turned slightly red.

'That was what you were to remind me about on the return trip,' he mumbled apologetically.

After the dinner, George walked outside to light his pipe and Daniel followed him out, intent on gaining more information about what had dropped out around the dinner table, but was distracted when Macarthur came out behind them and in a low voice full of conspiracy invited them to take a walk with him across the compound. There was what looked like an abandoned convict storehouse close to the fence, with a massive padlock on the solid wooden door. Macarthur took a large key from his tunic and opened it up, to reveal a collection of pots and pans, tubes and buckets, arranged in a very specific way.

George looked at it disparagingly. 'You brought us down here to admire your cooking equipment?' he asked.

'No — his still,' Daniel replied. 'I remember *those* from the tropics, too. Presumably you're converting some of the sugar into rum?'

'*Most* of it,' Macarthur confirmed with a self-satisfied grin. 'I'll be starting on the first batch in a few weeks, now that we have a decent supply of molasses. They're in another shed, towards the back. We ran an experiment a few weeks back, but the end product was almost undrinkable, so I gave it to George. Remember, George, I told you that it was to put on your garden vegetables, as a sort of concentrated compost? How did it go, by the way?'

'As a compost, it was a failure,' Daniel told him with a sideways scowl at George, 'but we both had hangovers for two days.'

'The next run should be much better,' Macarthur told them. 'Then I'll have the only rum manufacture in the colony. The governor doesn't know about it and I'd be obliged if you'd let me pick the appropriate time to tell him.'

'Surely he'd be pleased to see you adding to the colony's supply?' Daniel suggested.

Macarthur snorted. 'I didn't go to all this trouble just to supply the Commissary Store, even in exchange for shovels and pickaxes. You may not have noticed, but the last few ships to land in Sydney Cove have brought out settlers who aren't convicts. They've been given land by the governor, free of charge and they're hoping to farm it.'

'So?' George asked.

'So,' Macarthur repeated, 'put your hands in your pockets and tell me how much coin you have.'

'A few shillings,' George admitted, and Daniel nodded to suggest that this would be approximately the sum total of his loose change.

'And where did it come from?' Macarthur asked.

George had to think for a moment or two, before he replied. 'I think I brought it out here with me, now I come to think about it.'

'And you?' Macarthur asked Daniel.

'Me too,' Daniel admitted.

'Precisely,' Macarthur nodded triumphantly. 'And I'd be willing to bet that neither of you has found anything to spend it on in all the time since you landed, because you've been supplied with everything you need from the Commissary Store. The governor's obviously got it in mind to establish an entire new nation out here, starting with these "free settlers", as he calls them. The first few convicts will have completed their sentences in the next year or so and none of these people will be able to simply draw supplies from the Commissary Stores. How do you think they'll do business with each other?'

George and Daniel shook their heads, unable to answer.

Macarthur pressed his point. 'There's no Mint established here and unless we have some *very* expert forgers amongst the convicts, there'll be no banknotes either. The entire economy of this new society on which the governor has set his sights will be based on promissory notes, with no solid coinage or gold to back them up. All banking will be done in London and in the meantime we'll need a medium of exchange out here, for lesser men with no accounts in England. I propose to make rum that medium of exchange.'

'But won't it deteriorate, over time?' Daniel objected.

'Of course it will — either that or it'll be consumed. But by then it will have served its purpose. You don't keep your coins for ever, do you? You exchange them for other things that you need and then you consume those things. For example, when you were back in England, you'd buy yourself a fine meal for a shilling, then eat it. Out here, by the same process, you'll be able to acquire an agreed measure of grog for a week's work on someone's land, then exchange it for the food that your family needs. The farmer from who you buy that food then exchanges the rum for more seed or livestock and so on. Unless you actually consume the rum, you don't lose any of your capital and so it doesn't matter whether or not it goes off, because you never intend to drink it.'

'But at that rate,' Daniel said, 'the system you're suggesting could be established using anything as the means of exchange — wheat, for example, or chickens.'

'Yes,' Macarthur conceded, 'but the beauty of rum is that some people actually *do* want to drink it, particularly convicts. I'll pay them in rum, once they cease to be convicts, and I'll get all my work done for nothing.'

'But the governor pays their wages at the moment,' Daniel pointed out. 'At least, he gives the convicts an allowance from the Commissary Store.'

'A Commissary Store, let me remind you, that grows emptier by the week,' Macarthur countered. 'And as I just pointed out, over time these men who are now convicts will be looking for gainful employment, in a land that has no coinage or banknotes.'

'So you'll pay them in rum?' Daniel concluded.

'Once I get a regular supply of it up and running, certainly,' Macarthur replied.

'Can you produce enough of it, with the sugar you have available?' Daniel asked.

'Obviously not, once the system's fully operational,' Macarthur conceded. 'But from my India days I seem to recall that they do a nice line in the stuff and I can import it by the boatload, provided that I get a monopoly on the import.'

George had been looking uncomfortable as the dialogue between Macarthur and Daniel had continued and now he felt obliged to make an important point. 'I should, by rights, be reporting all this to the governor. I'm still his adjutant, despite Paterson trying to nudge me out of the way, and I'm sure his Excellency would not be amused to learn that you intend to set up an entire national economy based on "spirituous liquor", as he's fond of calling it, although he enjoys the odd tot himself.'

'Go ahead,' Macarthur smirked, 'but you'll find that whatever he orders will be quietly undermined by Grose or Paterson.'

'Paterson's still on Norfolk Island, surely?' George countered.

'Indeed he is,' Macarthur agreed, 'but he's been demoted and is furious that the governor's replaced him in the top office with his old friend King. Paterson's threatening to come back to Sydney and cause trouble, so I took the precaution of dealing directly with Grose himself.'

'You have Grose in your pocket?' George asked in disbelief.

Macarthur smiled unpleasantly. 'It was, I believe, Shakespeare who reminded us that "Misery doth acquaint a man with strange bedfellows". My theatre-loving wife is forever citing the phrases of our beloved Bard and that one's always stuck in my mind. Grose is like every career soldier — he's anxious to line his pockets before he takes his retirement pension and I've succeeded in bringing him into the scheme with a one quarter share of whatever we import. We begin with grog, then move on to sheep. Grose has all but persuaded the governor to give me some acreage up on the higher ground that's eminently suitable for sheep, but useless for growing crops.'

'So if I report all this, Grose will cover you if the governor tries to stop it?'

'The governor's lost his grip, surely you've realised that, since you deal with him daily? He's simply awaiting his recall papers and by the time they come through, the system will be fully operational. Whoever his replacement is will find that he can't stop the big ball rolling. I've already prevailed upon Grose to persuade his friends in high places in London to delay any replacement.'

'Why are you telling us all this and risking being reported?' Daniel asked.

'Because, Lieutenant, you and the captain here will all be part of this little community of ours before much longer and I'd rather that you be in on the arrangement than have to waste time deceiving you on a daily basis. As you will already have deduced, complaints upwards through the military chain will finish up on Grose's desk and his response will be to silence you, either by demotion on a trumped-up charge, or — dare I say it — with a little accident while out on patrol.'

'And from what I deduced over dinner,' Daniel replied with an accusing glare at George, 'my part in all this will be to keep the natives out of your hair.'

'I had no idea about the grog, I swear,' George told him, 'although I *was* aware of the plan to import sheep, since the governor's approved it.'

'When will the sheep be installed?' Daniel asked Macarthur, 'and will I be required to act as Shepherd-in-Chief, to guard your flock from the natives?'

'Regular but spasmodic patrols will be enough,' Macarthur replied, 'just so that the natives don't know where we are, or when we're likely to show up. As for the sheep, I need to await a suitable vessel whose captain can do the round trip —

preferably with the governor's knowledge and consent. Once we get up and running, we can charter vessels of our own to bring the rum from India and the sheep from Scotland or somewhere.'

'This is all going to take a few years,' George commented.

Macarthur smiled. 'Indeed it will, by which time you'll have a new lieutenant for your garrison here, while John Macarthur will be the wealthiest farmer in New South Wales.'

14

By the end of 1792, when Governor Phillip finally took his long-awaited departure back to England on the *Atlantic*, everything was going to plan. Grose had stepped up from lieutenant-governor to administrator of the colony and immediately began a policy of establishing the Corps as the supreme authority within New South Wales. He abolished the civil court system and replaced it with a military magistracy under the control of Captain Joseph Foveaux. He also bought the loyalty of the officers and men of the Corps by giving them generous land grants and supplying them with convict labour.

The convicts were fed, housed and clothed from a rapidly denuding Commissary Store and when their terms of imprisonment were nearing an end, Grose 'graciously' commuted those sentences with tickets of leave that made them free men. But with no money with which to buy a passage home, and many of them encumbered with wives, mistresses and children that they had not possessed when they first came out, they were obliged to seek employment on the large farms that were springing up in the west, run in the main by entrepreneurs such as John Macarthur who opted to remain in uniform, thereby continuing to draw military pay while putting their official duties in second place to their farming activities. Macarthur paid his free labourers exclusively in rum and sold the first year's crop of lambs to the Parramatta Commissary Store for which he had overall responsibility anyway.

Daniel, George, Esther and Martha were by then installed in houses inside the Parramatta Barracks complex, although

George had been granted some land to the south-west, half way between Parramatta and Botany Bay, in addition to other tracts of land further out, one of which he diplomatically named 'Bankstown', after one of those influential men in London who might be tempted to question the grant. He had acquired a few cattle, which he purchased from the Commissary in exchange for some of Macarthur's rum. He then arranged for a hut to be constructed on the Bankstown property, which he filled with convict farm labourers and dignified with the name of 'George's Hall'. It was well supplied with water from the adjacent Prospect Creek and guarded by a detachment of marines on permanent detail and under the notional supervision of First Lieutenant Daniel Bradbury.

This was not the only area of the country for which Daniel had responsibility, since his suspicions had been correct and George had allocated to him the 'external patrol' side of the Parramatta Barracks' daily activities. Every day Daniel was responsible for ensuring that groups of heavily armed marines were sent out into the surrounding countryside to flush out any native camps from which predatory raids could be conducted on the rapidly expanding flocks of sheep and herds of cattle. He rarely led these patrols himself and only showed his face among the natives when they appeared to be demonstrating their reluctance to move on when instructed by marines with fixed bayonets. Then, he would walk amongst the small clusters of native huts, calling out 'Friend', until someone reacted. That 'someone' was usually the leader of the particular clan encamped where they were not welcome, and Daniel soon learned that the outstretched palm of friendship worked more effectively than the threatened bayonet, particularly if that outstretched palm contained an item of worn convict clothing, or a jar of rum from Macarthur's still.

The only time Daniel wandered further afield was when he was sent to the north-west, in order to explore the possibility of opening new agricultural ventures in the land that lay between Parramatta and the Hawkesbury River. It had been known for some time that the river which in the west had been named 'Nepean' and which encircled the western expansion of Sydney, was the same river that was known, further north, as the Hawkesbury, and that the entire colony was therefore ringed by a freshwater source. Farms began to spring up in settlements known as Windsor, Castle Hill and Toongabbie, and where possible they were worked by convict labour under the supervision of men of the New South Wales Corps who were also their proprietors and were happy to pay their labourers in rum once their convict terms expired. They obtained the rum from Macarthur in exchange for some of the produce from their land, which in turn Macarthur fed to the labourers on his own rapidly expanding sheep farm.

Esther and Martha had settled down reasonably comfortably to barracks life and were relieved to be living behind brick walls rather than in wooden huts. Their children appeared to be thriving and there was a child community of sorts within the barracks which Daniel all but commanded, given John Macarthur's daily excursions to his nearby sheep enterprise, with its own convict hut, which he had named 'Elizabeth Farm', not that the lady after whom it was named seemed keen to visit it.

Elizabeth Macarthur had taken immediately to Martha, although she had no idea of her background, or indeed of Esther's. She had assumed that, being officer's wives like herself, they were from a 'certain position' in society and her snobbery gleamed out like the glass jewellery she always wore to formal dinners at the Barracks. When first introduced to

Martha over drinks in the 'Officer's Reading Room' (her own term for the collection of cracked leather armchairs in which off-duty officers like George, John and Daniel could skim in a desultory manner through London newspapers at least a year old), Elizabeth had immediately announced her life-long love of the theatre and had demanded to know which plays were Martha's favourites.

Faking a lengthy and languid trip through her pretended vast memory of the productions in which she had appeared, which in fact gave her time to think quickly, Martha replied, in a wonderful imitation of a slightly bored doyen of the footlights, 'Probably the Restoration Comedies — particularly the works of Mr. Congreve. Of course, one always aspires to play Lady Macbeth, or perhaps even Ophelia, but such opportunities are rarely afforded to one in Drury Lane. However, I must own that it has been a relief to come out here, where the crowds are not always waiting outside the stage door and gentlemen of *quite* the wrong sort are not always inviting one out to dinner.'

'I thought you were overdoing it a little,' Daniel laughed as he recalled the conversation. They were sitting with George and Esther in the front room of their half of the large brick house, divided into two separate residences, each with two rooms and with a communicating internal door between the two front rooms, for ease of access between the two families when the weather was too inclement to permit a short trip outside.

'I enjoyed myself,' Martha admitted, 'and I think that I succeeded in fooling her.'

'She thoroughly deserved it anyway, pompous old crow that she is,' Esther responded. Esther's first few conversations with Elizabeth had been barely civil, as the two proud women mentally prowled round each other like sniffing dogs. It was one of those instant dislikes of which people are capable without being able to explain why, but Esther was convinced that Elizabeth was trying to put her in her place. Elizabeth was clearly jealous of Esther's friendship with Martha, who Elizabeth believed to be a successful former London actress and was setting out to prove that she was a 'step above' Esther. Elizabeth had quizzed her almost incessantly about her origins, no doubt alerted by her dark features to the possibility that she might be Jewish and Esther had announced that prior to marrying George, her name had been 'Juliano' and that her ancestry was Spanish and possibly of the nobility.

'It really is *quite* tragic when noble persons are reduced to positions of such wretchedness that they are obliged to marry into even the respectable professions,' Elizabeth had cooed cattily, to which Esther had retorted, with a face set like a fire iron, 'Yes, but at least they have the consolation of pure blood in their ancestry, which I find is a very competent antidote to the boredom of public service, or the lack of inherent intellect which one finds in so many of the service wives with whom one is obliged to converse.'

They had now been there for a year and there was no news of any replacement governor. The reason why Grose had paid them all a visit had been to appoint John Macarthur officially as his Superintendent of Public Works and Paymaster for the entire New South Wales Corps. However, Macarthur had not been promoted in rank and he and Daniel were still at first lieutenant level, neither having precedence over the other. But Grose had left them in no doubt that he required Daniel to do the real soldiering, leaving Macarthur to promote his several and various business schemes. The colony was rapidly reverting to what it had been at the very beginning — a hierarchy of officers presiding over a prison regime in which convicts were employed as cheap labour, while the senior officers took every opportunity to benefit financially, sexually and socially.

This was all put under threat when Grose returned to England in December 1794 due to ill health and William Paterson returned from Norfolk Island to assume temporary command of the colony in the absence of any incoming governor. Everyone knew that Major Paterson, as he had now become in order to outrank George, would not be in charge forever and nobody knew that more clearly than Paterson himself, with the result that he tried to put paid to the rapidly burgeoning monopoly that his officers out west were virtually controlling without any assistance from him. Not only was he not benefitting from it personally, but Paterson was acutely aware that one day in the immediate future he would have to explain the state of the colony to a new governor. He forbade the almost exclusive use of sugar and grain for distillation in the many 'sly grog' huts that the marines were blatantly operating, and let it be known that any officer discovered to have imported cheap rum from anywhere would be court-martialled.

Then news came, via the *Batavia*, which delivered over five hundred new 'free' settlers in January 1795, that a new governor would be arriving later that year. His name was John Hunter and despatches sent to Paterson by the governor-elect and shared by Paterson with George Johnston, also advised those in Sydney that Hunter's orders were to develop New South Wales into a fully functional English colony and reduce the number of convicts to a minimum. Every encouragement was to be given to the free settlers who were now arriving on every boat; they were to be given land grants and they were to be encouraged to establish businesses, particularly of a farming or trading nature. The one glimmer of light was a 'whisper' from 'an influential source' that Hunter had expressed a wish to have Captain George Johnston as his *aide-de-camp*.

They all met around the main table in the Officers' Mess inside the barracks, to discuss how they were to best position themselves to withstand this challenge to their growing commercial dominance of the settlement, and in particular the now almost universal use of distilled liquor and principally rum, as a form of currency. To make matters worse, several wet seasons had reduced the sugar cane and grain harvests.

'As I see it,' Macarthur said, 'we need to increase the supply of rum threefold, so that we have a stranglehold on the entire economy before Hunter even gets here. I'm led to believe that it may still be cheaply obtained in India. Paterson will of course wash his hands of the whole business if he finds out, but George will be on hand to advise that doddering old fool Hunter that the colony's more easily governed this way and that the economic expansion that London's demanding cannot occur without a common currency. Having a ready supply of rum will be like being in charge of the Royal Mint back home.'

'Easier said than done,' George observed sadly. 'We can hardly commission a ship to India without risking a court martial. It would need to be done surreptitiously, by someone who can't be linked back to us in any way. Can anyone think of such a man?'

'Why does it have to be a man?' Daniel asked. The other two looked at him in surprise, as he explained. 'We need someone to pretend to be someone they aren't — or at least, someone unconnected with the marines in any way. No one would suspect a woman of being a marine officer and I happen to be married to the best actress we have in the colony.'

George's eyebrows shot up in excitement. 'Do you think she'd agree?'

'Why not? She's always complaining about how bored she is sitting at home, nursing a young child and staring at the wall. All we have to do is provide the right setting for her. First of all, we need to choose the ship. Does anyone happen to know if the *Batavia* has a return cargo, or any fresh charterparty?'

'According to Paterson,' George was able to reveal, 'she's on permanent charter to the Admiralty. However, I'm sure the captain could be persuaded to do an extra run to India without the knowledge of his masters in London, if the money's right.'

'Talking of money,' Daniel chipped in, 'where do you propose to get the sum you'll need for an entire boatload from India?'

Macarthur smiled and tapped his nose. 'You're talking to the Paymaster-General of the New South Wales Corps, remember. We have a considerable amount of ready currency in the secure armoury, where we keep anything of value. At the last count we had almost five thousand sovereigns and I calculate that we could fill an entire vessel with cheap Indian gut-rot for that price. All we need is to get to the captain and persuade him to do the run without revealing who the real purchasers are.'

George turned to Daniel. 'Do you reckon Martha's up to it?'

Daniel grinned back. 'You've seen her in action, George. She had me fooled for several weeks and she fooled an entire court-martial. Let's just work out who we want her to pretend to be, then point her at the target.'

A week later, Richard Mayhew, master of the *Batavia*, was surprised to be advised by his boatswain that two ladies had come aboard the vessel where she lay at anchor in Sydney Cove and were anxious to speak with him. He rose from behind his desk in the captain's cabin as the ladies were ushered in, one of them a very attractive young lady with masses of black hair demurely tied under a black bonnet and the other a more matronly looking companion whose face was covered by a dark veil until she lifted it to reveal a solemn face and dark, penetrating eyes. Both women were dressed all in black and it was the older looking of them who spoke first.

'Permit me to introduce my sister-in-law Matilda Mason, widow of my late brother Isaac Mason. She has a business proposition for you.'

Martha sniffed and wiped her eyes with her glove, which was smeared with dark pepper to make more tears flow freely. 'Please forgive my intrusion into your rest while at anchor, but I have need of your vessel if I am to retain my fortune — or, rather, that of my late husband.'

'It's no hardship to be entertaining two such attractive ladies in my cabin,' Mayhew replied, already intrigued. 'How may I be of service to you?'

Martha wiped her eyes again to ensure a ready flow of tears, while Esther placed a consoling arm around her as the pretence proceeded.

'My husband and I came out here last year,' Martha explained. 'Isaac is — sorry, *was* — a leading dealer in spirits in London, where we had several warehouses in Rotherhithe. He was hoping to establish a branch of his office out here in this promising new land and to that end brought out with him a considerable sum of money with which to purchase rum from India. He already had it promised to several prominent persons here in Sydney and his business would suffer great loss of prestige and commercial respect were he to fail to deliver. He had intended to charter a suitable vessel over here to honour the many contracts he had made, but sadly he died of a fever he contracted on board during our passage out here. Pardon me,' she added for effect, as she appeared to break down with the emotional strain and Esther placed a consoling hand on her arm before looking back at Mayhew.

'We require your vessel in order to honour the contract. It is, I am informed, a relatively short crossing and an easy one in calm weather. We would require you to source, pay for and bring back a consignment of rum from Calcutta. We would obviously provide you with the money for the purchase and could offer you a further five hundred pounds — to be divided between you and your crew — for a voyage that would take you two months at the most, if the advice I have received is correct. There might be other such ladings in the future, but I am led to believe that you are required to return to Portsmouth.'

'Five hundred pounds, you say? That would be acceptable,' Mayhew replied, trying not to reveal by his facial expression that he would have been prepared to undertake the commission for half that amount. 'When shall the money come aboard and where in Calcutta shall I source the cargo?'

'The choice of cargo must be yours,' Martha replied, 'although as a seagoing man I feel sure that we may rely on your own judgment regarding its quality. As for the money, five thousand sovereigns may be brought aboard as soon as you can moor your vessel upstream at the Parramatta Wharf — shall we say in two days' time? I will have two of my late husband's men bring it on board and guard it during the voyage. No disrespect to yourself, but they will of course be heavily armed.'

'I enjoyed that,' Esther confessed as the two women were being rowed back across the harbour by six convicts detailed for the task from Macarthur's farm and paid with rum.

Martha chuckled. 'I'm afraid you betrayed yourself as a budding actress, Esther. When I launch my first production, you will undoubtedly be playing a leading role.'

The following evening, Sergeant Milligan and Private Bush, handpicked from Daniel's 'A Company', but wearing civilian clothing, climbed aboard the *Batavia* carrying a heavy box between them, which they guarded all the way to Calcutta. On the way back, they relaxed and enjoyed a permanent state of inebriation.

15

The new governor finally arrived in September 1795, allowing Major Paterson to sail back to London on the returning vessel, to some much-needed sick leave after the pressure of running the colony for the best part of two years. His was not the only promotion, since Governor Hunter used his first visit to Parramatta to authorise the promotion of John Macarthur to the rank of Captain, while establishing his working relationship with George, as his *aide-de-camp*, by promoting him to Major.

The strategic significance of the developments to the west of Sydney were not lost on him and he insisted that George give priority to the military supervision of these, while also ensuring that sufficient officers remained in Sydney to maintain law and order there. The departure of Major Paterson had left George as the senior military officer in the colony and the new governor appeared to be unaware that Major Johnston had previously only been responsible for Parramatta, a state of ignorance that George did nothing to dispel. Governor Hunter was also anxious to ensure that key figures in his administration were fully aware of what he (which meant London) was expecting of them all.

'I answer directly to the Duke of Portland,' he told George and Macarthur during their first meeting in the Parramatta Barracks, 'and he's adamant that we reduce the cost of running the colony.'

'By reducing the number of convicts dependent on the Commissary Stores, you mean?' Macarthur asked with a smile.

'Precisely,' Governor Hunter replied, 'which is why I'm so pleased to see so much development taking place out here without the need for direct convict labour. As far as I've been able to calculate from the somewhat haphazard records that my predecessor left behind him, only some forty per cent of the labourers and craftsmen out here are receiving sustenance direct from the Store. How do you pay the rest — the ones who are free settlers for one reason or another?'

'Obviously it's difficult, with the shortage of actual coinage in circulation,' Macarthur explained, 'but in the main they seem to be content to be paid in kind.'

'You mean rum?' Hunter asked, his face clouding slightly. 'Paterson was forever bombarding London with complaints about you paying emancipates with rum and other liquor.'

'With respect,' George chimed in, 'Major Paterson only saw things with Sydney eyes. He was also against so many convicts becoming emancipated, because he wanted to retain the old ways, with convicts guarded by a military elite. Out here we have to be more practical, and men who are working for themselves, rather than labouring under the supervision of a marine with a bayonet, are likely to be far more productive. Emancipation also serves the purpose required by London, of reducing the direct cost of the colony, although — as you have no doubt already pointed out to them — the more convicts they send out here, the greater the strain on the Commissary and the greater the cost to the colony. But they save money and overcrowding in English gaols, as you have no doubt *also* pointed out.'

'But even so,' Hunter argued, 'I can hardly report to Portland that we have a healthy and developing economy based entirely on rum as a medium of exchange. I have in mind opening a Mint and launching our own currency.'

A look of alarm flashed briefly across Macarthur's face. 'We don't rely exclusively on rum, Governor,' he hastened to explain. 'Out there we have several growing sheep stations and George here has recently gone into cattle.'

Hunter snorted derisively. 'Even less suitable, I would have thought. If a man does a day's work for you, do you give him half a sheep's leg in payment? For a week's wages, will he get an entire cow's arse?'

'Obviously not,' Macarthur explained patiently. 'But I have hopes of being able to sell my sheep to those free settlers who're beginning to farm out here. They've brought coinage out with them, expecting to pay their way in the English manner and those coins will, by those means, begin circulating around the colony. The more sheep — and for that matter, cattle — the more money in circulation and the less need for you to open a Mint, which surely cannot be your highest priority anyway.'

'No indeed,' Hunter confirmed. 'We need a new hospital and barracks complex long before then and I have in mind a new Governor's Mansion, perhaps out along the roadway just outside here.'

'I'll look into that immediately, Governor,' Macarthur assured him, 'but might I also ask if the next supply ship master could be instructed to find me some more grazing stock? The sheep we have at present are quite adequate, since I've managed to cross some hardy Bengal ewes with Irish rams that produce a pretty fine wool. But if I can increase and improve the breeding stock, I may soon be able to export some of my wool back to England, which will of course bring more coinage into the colony. They're also not bad to eat, as you'll discover at dinner time.'

'Very well, you have my authority for that,' Hunter told him. 'But I also need to make better arrangements for you to carry out your duties for me in Sydney, George,' he added, turning to another matter close to his immediate needs. 'You already have a considerable amount of land to the south of the Cove, but there's a patch in between, just to the south-west of the harbour itself. I'm granting you another hundred acres out there on the water, along with a cutter and crew all of your own. It's adjacent to the land you already own and that way you'll be able to attend at Governor's Mansion in Sydney whenever you're required. You can also follow Macarthur's splendid example and open up a farm; we need cattle and horses, rather than more sheep, but I'll leave that to you. I'll allocate a dozen convicts to build you a house wherever you see fit.'

'Thank you, Governor,' George replied, 'Esther *will* be pleased.'

'Remember, it's in order that you can carry out your duties as my *aide-de-camp* more efficiently,' Hunter reminded him. 'It should not be seen as a precedent by any of your men. Talking of whom, who have you detailed to escort me to the Government Farm? I want to get that out of the way before we sit down to dinner.'

'First Lieutenant Bradbury, sir, since he's the one who polices it on a daily basis. I'll just have him sent for.'

Daniel had been waiting outside, somewhat aggrieved that he hadn't been allowed to attend the briefing with the governor and seemed to have been demoted to guide duties for the old buffer who looked as if he would barely survive the brisk hour's ride out to Castle Hill, where a new government farm had been established to replace the experimental one that James Ruse had pioneered just across the new road from the barracks. Once it was known what grew best, one of the last actions of the outgoing colonial caretaker Paterson had been to establish what amounted to a strict convict compound up to the north, where grain and root crops were being successfully raised and sent back to the Commissary Store.

Daniel had complained about the remoteness of the place and the practical difficulties involved in maintaining an adequate number of Corps personnel to hold down a largely mutinous bunch of recalcitrant convicts, who appeared to him to have been selected solely on the basis of their disrespect for authority. The men he stationed out there were constantly complaining and none of them was prepared to settle out there with a wife and family, given the lecherous looks that the convicts gave to any female who went near the place.

Daniel had commissioned the two best mounts that the barracks possessed, but even so the governor was red in the face, sweating heavily and clearly somewhat testy, when they finally breasted the hill that led to the guardhouse and compound, inside which men could be seen hoeing the land to clear weeds from between the lines of grain crops, or hacking down the remaining trees so as to enable further expansion once their roots had been grubbed out.

'How many men here, Lieutenant?'

'Two sergeants and eight privates, working alternate shifts, sir.'

'I meant *convicts*, you fool,' Hunter admonished him.

Daniel swallowed the urge to knock the miserable old idiot off his horse and breathed deeply before replying. 'At the last count, seventy-two, sir. And a pretty hard bunch they are, too. My men are in constant fear of a mass uprising of some sort, which is why I keep the place so heavily garrisoned.'

'You can hardly blame the convicts for resenting their lot in life, particularly in this God-forsaken hole. Is this the hottest it gets?' Hunter asked, removing his hat and mopping his brow.

'No, sir,' Daniel replied with a hint of a smirk. 'It's only October and by January it'll be twice as hot and as steamy as the tropics. Not a good place to be visiting once the full summer sets in.'

'I hope *never* to have to visit again,' Hunter retorted, 'but since I'm here anyway and can see for myself what a miserable dump it is, you'd better show me around.'

'Sergeant Bellamy is waiting to do that, sir,' Daniel replied, mentally wishing his sergeant the best of luck. 'I'll water our horses and get them rubbed down.'

'You might want to do that for the both of *us*, while you're at it,' Hunter grumbled.

The return journey was no more enjoyable and Daniel was happy to leave the governor to enjoy a late dinner with George and Macarthur and return to his house, where the atmosphere of late had been little better. Martha clearly had something on her mind and whatever it was that was bothering her had made her somewhat short in her manner towards him. Not cold — just brisk and almost business-like, as if avoiding the need to engage in any meaningful conversation.

Daniel took a deep breath and went inside, where Martha was just lifting a pot of soup from the stove.

'It's a bit hot for soup today,' Daniel remarked by way of a conversation opener.

Martha snorted in that way of hers lately. 'Sorry it's not oysters and champagne, but the Commissary had just run out. The bread's yesterday's as well — I couldn't get time to cross the parade square, what with Matthew throwing his toys everywhere whenever I gave them to him, in the hope that he'd settle down. And if I try to carry him these days, he just bawls and screams to be put down to walk, then I have to worry that he'll fall over and cut himself or something. God forbid that I have to present him at that hospital next door.'

'It's not easy, I know,' Daniel offered by way of consolation.

Martha slammed the soup pot back on the stove, put her hands on her hips in a defiant gesture and said, 'You know *nothing*, Daniel! You don't have to spend every day in this dump of a house, with a child that's determined to find every possible way of hurting himself, wondering what on earth I can cook that isn't made from lentils, cabbage, potatoes or John's sheep. So don't tell me "you know", because you *don't!*'

Daniel's jaw dropped. He knew his wife had spirit, as she had demonstrated before their marriage, but she had never turned on him like this since before their first night together. Nor had she ever voiced any discontent over their living conditions, seemingly happy to be a wife and mother living at government expense, watching their child grow up in a safe and loving environment. He was completely dumbstruck as he watched her face slowly crease, first in regret, then in supplication, then in total misery as she sank down in the chair, laid her head on the table and cried bitter tears of remorse and self-pity.

Daniel walked slowly across to her and tentatively stretched a hand onto her shoulder, expecting it to be shaken off angrily. Instead she gripped it hard, lifted her head, kissed the hand, then gasped out a few words. 'Darling — so sorry — you don't deserve it — forgive me.' The tears still ran down her red face as she pulled him down on the chair next to her and folded him in her arms. '*Please* tell me you still love me and I haven't ruined everything.'

He caressed her long black locks, matted with sweat and badly needing a comb. 'I think I loved you the day I found you at the bottom of that pile of women on deck and I'll love you till the day I die, whatever you do or say, but clearly something's wrong and has been for several weeks, so now would be a good time to tell me all about it.'

She looked up into his eyes and, half-laughing and half-crying, told him, 'I'm expecting again.'

Daniel's eyes widened and a smile lit up his face. From total despair to ecstatic happiness in the space of less than a minute, it was certainly not boring being married to Martha. The smile turned into his trademark grin as he reached down and gently stroked her stomach. 'Hello there, Mark,' he joked.

'It could be a girl,' she reminded him.

He sat back and looked at her thoughtfully. 'I realise that you went through a bad time giving birth to Matthew, but at least we have the hospital doctor at hand here and Sarah seems to know what she's doing...'

Martha put her fingers to his lips to silence the flow of reassurance. 'I wasn't upset just because I'm pregnant — in fact it's the best thing that's happened all year. But that's the point, Daniel — it's the *only* thing that's happened all year. You really do have no idea what it's like being stuck in this tiny prison, day after day, week after week, with only Matthew for company. Even Esther seems to be missing most of the time, visiting the farms with George.'

'You need an interest — a hobby,' Daniel suggested.

Martha laughed hollowly. 'Typical man! Buy the little wifey a tapestry to work, encourage her to read a riveting novel, buy her a musical instrument to practice on. Meanwhile, you go out there every day, doing your soldiering. Every day's different for you — you don't have the soul-crushing boredom of routine, the misery of preparing the same meals week in and week out.'

'What about that theatre that Elizabeth wants you to start up?'

There was another hollow laugh as Martha stood up and stirred the soup with the ladle that she wrapped in a cloth before handling it. She looked back at Daniel over her shoulder. 'If anything would be likely to tip me over the edge it's the thought of having to spend time with that snooty cow Elizabeth Macarthur. She's been promoted from "tedious" to "insufferable" since John got *his* promotion and she never stops going on about their "estate" in Rose Hill, as if it wasn't just half a mile down the road. Every time you fail to avoid her company, she bleats on about the latest addition to the new house out there on Elizabeth Farm — "My darling John named it after me, you know",' — she added, in a perfect impersonation of the woman that made Daniel laugh.

'I just wish there was something I could do to brighten your day,' he said.

'There is,' Martha replied, nodding at where Matthew had fallen asleep under the table where he'd crawled during the earlier argument. 'You've already got me pregnant, so we've got nothing to lose. Mary Murphy — the fallen convent girl — would be mightily impressed if you'd lead her by the hand into the bed in the next room.'

16

Daniel was even more apprehensive of Martha's fragile state of mind when George announced that he and Esther would be moving out from next door into the house that the governor had commissioned for them, at government expense, on their newly acquired additional land, which George had christened 'Annandale' in honour of his birthplace in the Scottish Borders. The only compensation was that John Macarthur had recently acquired, through the medium of a supply ship sent by the governor to Cape Town, a hold full of pure Merino lambs that had originated in Spain and had been purchased from the widow of their owner. His fleece count promised to be three times greater than previously and when the first fleeces were successfully sold by sample to a London dealer, John and Elizabeth moved out from the barracks, in great pomp, to Elizabeth Farm, leaving Daniel and Martha to take over the Barracks Commander's three-roomed house.

Macarthur was still in notional command of the outpost, however, and Daniel had cause to be grateful that it was Macarthur who was called upon to deal, in his official capacity, with an incident involving some of his men at the Dawes Point cottage of John Baughan, a convict whose skills as a carpenter had earned him considerable favour with Francis Grose, to the extent that he had been allowed to erect and live in a cottage in a very desirable area of Sydney while constructing a mill under marine guard.

However, one of the marines guarding him — Jacob Talbot — was also an emancipated convict, although no one except the two men in question was aware that while they had both been convicts, Baughan and Talbot had become sworn enemies. Baughan seized his opportunity when he found Talbot asleep on night duty outside his cottage and stole his musket, which he returned to the lieutenant of the Sydney Guard. Talbot was placed in irons awaiting disciplinary proceedings, but contrived to get a message through to his former colleagues in Parramatta, who marched by night to Baughan's cottage and totally demolished it, Baughan himself barely escaping with his life.

Everyone waited for the predictable court-martials of those responsible and their likely hanging or flogging. Macarthur was hastily consulted and offered total financial compensation to the aggrieved Baughan, which he accepted. The governor, rather than risk further confrontation with Macarthur, whose commercial co-operation was essential for the efficient running of the colony, withdrew the warrants of arrest that had been issued against the perpetrators on the ground that sufficient justice had been done, while at the same time issuing a proclamation that any further such behaviour — on *anyone's* part — would be regarded as an act of mutiny, with capital consequences.

But a precedent had clearly been set and the writing was writ large on the wall. The Corps was arguably beyond the control of the governor, as several prominent citizens in the colony lost no time in advising the Duke of Portland in despatches sent to London by the next returning vessel. Portland responded by ordering Hunter to rein in the New South Wales Corps and to recruit companies of 'Volunteers' to assist the fulltime professional soldiers should the colony come under attack, either from natives who were increasingly expressing their discontent at what they regarded as the encroaching occupation of their traditional lands, or from convict uprisings.

Hunter passed these instruction on to his *aide-de-camp* George Johnston, who happily delegated the task to officers beneath him in Sydney, but told Macarthur to do as he thought best, fearful that Macarthur would simply pass the order down the line to the already overworked and over-stretched Daniel, who was about to become a father for the second time and whose wife was beginning to crack under the strain of barracks life.

Macarthur, for his part and under pressure from his own socially ambitious wife, was rapidly becoming the wealthiest man in the colony, thanks to the virtual monopoly he enjoyed over rum imports from India and other parts of Asia and supplies of mutton to the Commissary Store at a price that was only just below what it would have to pay were it to import the carcasses from England or South Africa, on fleets whose inadequate refrigeration techniques often resulted in the ships containing long-dead mutton being smelt before they were seen. There were only two such experiments before the scheme was abandoned and in the meantime Elizabeth Farm fleeces were fetching top prices in Leeds and Manchester, given their superior quality. The wealth that these exchanges created enabled Macarthur to establish a crude form of bank before any were established in the settlement, since he could write bills of exchange and promissory notes against his 'futures' expectations in the English markets.

Free settlers who had moved to the colony in the hope of making their own fortunes resented George Johnston almost as much as they did John Macarthur, because of George's large estates and rapidly increasing cattle herds that competed for grazing acreage not only with those of the would-be cattle barons among the emigrants, but also with the government herds that were threatening to wander beyond the slim fences of the Government Farm and were regularly being speared by wandering native tribes who treated the convict-staffed establishment as a free larder. Letter after angry letter reached the Duke of Portland in London and at the suggestion of Sir Joseph Banks he consulted Banks's protégé William Paterson, who was no great admirer of Johnston, Macarthur and their cronies.

Paterson advised Portland that Hunter was clearly not capable of enforcing his authority over the Corps and that in particular there was no immediate hope of any end to the monopolistic grip over the supply of liquor in the colony being exercised by 'The Rum Corps' as they were nicknamed in Whitehall. Paterson was made up to Lieutenant-Colonel and instructed to pack his sea chest in anticipation of a return to New South Wales to preside over the replacement of one governor by another.

In November 1799, Paterson stepped onto the wharf at Sydney as the new Commandant of the New South Wales Corps, determined to enforce his instructions from London to break the growing economic power of the Corps by restraining the trading activities of its officers. He also carried Banks's verbal instructions to demean the efforts of Hunter's administration, so that Banks could replace him with his own nominee for the post, and every vessel that left Sydney contained letters of complaint that were written in order to exaggerate the crisis in the eyes of those reading them in London.

In particular, Paterson criticised the commercial stranglehold over the colony that the officers beneath him had been allowed to strengthen during Hunter's watch, which he — Paterson — was having severe difficulty in reducing. He also reported unfavourably on the lax treatment of Irish convicts who had been sent out as political prisoners following the recent rebellion in their home country and who Hunter had sent out west, where they were proving difficult for the Parramatta soldiers under Daniel to hold down and usefully employ in government schemes.

That was all the ammunition that Banks required and less than a year later, Philip Gidley King, former Lieutenant-Governor of Norfolk Island and chosen favourite of Banks, arrived with a commission to replace Hunter signed by the Duke of Portland, Hunter's previous champion, who had lost the political fight at the London end.

In a well-choreographed move, Hunter's departure was accompanied by the appointment of Paterson as Lieutenant-Governor and to him fell the detailed responsibility for bringing down the Corps, now symbolised by George Johnston and John Macarthur. In an attempt to isolate Macarthur and prevent him from being assisted too closely by George, Paterson insisted that since George was still the governor's *aide-de-camp* anyway and was required to visit the governor's domain every day, he should also be given responsibility for the day-to-day protection of the governor, in addition to his existing duties in Parramatta.

When George complained, Paterson reminded him that it was high time that Macarthur earned his military salary out there and spent less time on his sheep. Governor King also began his own policy of economic warfare with the military monopolists, establishing a public warehouse in which goods were imported from England and offered for resale to the free settlers at prices that ensured only a modest profit, but which allowed more coinage to circulate freely in the colony, in an effort to break the now almost traditional valuation of everyday goods and services in terms of rum or animal flesh. He also began the construction of a brewery to appeal to the tastes of those who would prefer not to drink spirits, while seeking to impose standard measures for basic goods and opening a government printing works in which promissory notes could be produced, in order to counter the increasing number of forgeries. Finally, he imported considerable herds of both cattle and sheep, which he installed on government farms, or sold to settlers at prices considerably lower than those charged by Macarthur and George.

He also encouraged the increased extraction of coal from the recently opened mines in the valley named 'Hunter' after his predecessor, in order that it might be exported back to England to raise more coinage for circulation in the colony. More and more free settlers were given large land grants and supplied with livestock on credit, in the hope of bringing down the market price of slaughtered beasts.

Before long there was a widening three-way rift between the military monopolists, the free settlers and the emancipated convicts who were flooding onto the employment market and in some cases being recruited into the volunteer regiments of 'Loyal Associations', to ensure that the Corps were not the only ones upon whom the community relied for its security.

In the main, George and Macarthur regarded these policies with tolerant amusement. They were still the largest pastoralists in the settlement and the sheer numbers of animal carcasses that they could send to market at their own chosen prices kept up their own growth in personal wealth, to the point at which their soldiers' salaries were almost an irrelevance. The significance of their commissions was no longer the incomes they generated, but the positions of physical power that they occupied, in command of fully trained and operational fighting men who were the first line of defence against the natives and the only legitimate means of holding down the diminishing number of convicts working on the government schemes. It was a rapidly changing society, but George, Macarthur and their senior officers were still at the top end of it.

It wasn't long before George's mansion in Annandale was completed by convict labour urged on to greater efforts by weekly bonuses of 'fly' rum from one or other of Macarthur's stills and paid for by George in cattle, which were added to the grazing stocks at Elizabeth Farm. Both men could afford to reward others in return for carrying out their military duties and they slowly grew less fit as they exchanged a daily routine of marching men up and down for the easier task of sitting on long verandas sipping rum cocktails and watching convict labour herding their flocks.

All of this imposed a considerable additional burden on Daniel, which became almost intolerable when Martha announced that Esther had invited her and the children to transfer to the more palatial surroundings of 'George's Hall', the six room mansion on the banks of Prospect Creek in Annandale, where Martha had given birth to Rebecca, their second child, in 1799. When Esther had discovered shortly afterwards that she was also again with child, Martha grasped the excuse to stay on and look after her, while allowing Matthew to experience his early childhood days in the company of Esther's two boys, George Junior and Robert. Even after the birth of Esther's third son David, Martha had employed one excuse after another to delay returning to the gaunt barracks house in Parramatta and Daniel had reverted to an almost bachelor existence as he continued to supervise the garrison that Macarthur had long since abandoned for Elizabeth Farm.

George showed only passing interest in the difficulties that Daniel was experiencing in holding down a mutinous crew of

Irish political convicts employed at the Government Farm at Castle Hill. Even when armed, his men would only enforce their authority over the convict labourers if they were in pairs and George's only advice to Daniel was to ensure that every refusal to obey orders was met with a flogging or a withdrawal of food and drink. This just made the convicts more resentful and the hatred that gleamed from their eyes resulted in fewer and fewer of Daniel's detachment being prepared to accept allocation to the Government Farm. Not only were the convicts on the point of mutiny — so were Daniel's men and he was seriously contemplating resigning his commission and moving to a free-holding with Martha and the children, an option that was greeted by Martha, when he put it to her, with a snort of dismissal and a reminder that she was more comfortably established in her new existence than she had ever been at any time in her life.

Daniel reverted to living in a barracks house in Parramatta and George was obliged to take back overall command of the Corps when Paterson succumbed yet again to the heat and humidity and was obliged to relinquish daily responsibility for military matters. With no 'buffer' between the governor and his arrogant military officers, relations between the civil administration and the military deteriorated further, to the point at which the soldiers would do only what their officers told them directly, while the officers followed Paterson's precedent and began penning letters to London, complaining hypocritically about King's inability to manage a developing community.

But the following year, Governor King had every reason to be thankful that he still had fighting men who were determined not to let the convicts take over, and Daniel found himself at the very centre of events.

17

Daniel came instantly awake when a private burst into his bedroom in the Commander's house that he was once again occupying at the Barracks, while Macarthur was officially on overseas leave.

'Sir, we have a full-scale uprising on our hands!' the private shouted, his voice driven by adrenalin and tense with fear. 'Down at the Government Farm — I've sent out word for the volunteer detachment to arm themselves and come to the Barracks and all our fulltime men are assembling on the Parade Square.'

Daniel shook his head to clear his thoughts and remembered George. 'Send a fast horse back to Annandale and summon Major Johnston from his bed. Tell the men I'll be out in five minutes.'

'Yes, sir,' the private replied as he headed back outside.

All that they could tell him, once Daniel ran out to take command of his detachment, was that a private from the Government Farm detail out at Castle Hill had staggered into the guardhouse, badly wounded and severely bruised after falling off his horse as he swerved it through the Barracks gates. He had managed to gasp a few words, before losing consciousness and being left where he fell so that he could be attended to by hospital staff. So far as could be made out, the convicts had overpowered the almost token guard at the Castle Hill farm and were believed to be heading for the Commissary Store at Parramatta in order to acquire weapons and other supplies. What they were intending to do next was anyone's guess.

While Daniel was wondering how best to deal with the challenge, men from the local volunteer battalion that had been raised among local farmers and other emancipated convicts began arriving in their makeshift uniforms, carrying muskets, swords and other rudimentary fighting implements. Daniel assigned to them the obvious first task of securing the Barracks entrance against any attempt to break through it in order to gain access to the Commissary, then told his own fulltime marine infantry to load their own muskets and line up in marching formation, in anticipation of breaking out of the Barracks to attack any convict force that threatened to get beyond the volunteers at the gate.

He was unsure of who he might be dealing with, but could hazard a guess that somewhere behind this uprising was an Irish convict named Philip Cunningham, who had been trouble since the day he had been consigned to the unpopular Government Farm in the latest instalment of his life sentence for his part in the Irish Rebellion of 1798. At Castle Hill, Cunningham had flaunted his iconic status among his fellow convicts and had been a constant threat to the somewhat lax security there, given the reluctance of the marine guard to enforce their strict orders for fear that they would be overpowered and slaughtered by the wild Irishman and his fellow rebel companion William Johnston. What passed for a garrison at Castle Hill had also been supplemented by emancipated convicts who were now notionally guarding their former fellow prisoners and fell easy prey to the powerful and charismatic Irishman who talked of escape, rebellion, a ship to China and an Irish Republic in the convict colony.

It was approaching midnight before the breathless messenger disturbed the sleep of everyone at Annandale, Esther and Martha fearfully gathering their children around them as they listened to the news of the convict mob marching on Parramatta. Martha was beside herself with panic when she realised that Daniel was now the only senior officer between the uprising and Sydney and she pleaded with George to send reinforcements immediately. Instead, George gave the trooper a glass of beer and a beef sandwich, then ordered him to take his own boat across the nearby harbour to alert Governor King.

The women had taken time to dress themselves properly and hide the children, for their own safety, in a back room, by the time that Governor King arrived with a small escort.

'I've put the entire colony under martial law, Major,' he told George as he shook his head at the glass of wine offered to him by Esther. 'I've also left word for Lieutenant Dickson at the Sydney Barracks to raise a *posse comitatus* and I'm riding out immediately to Parramatta with Miles and Potter to review the situation for myself. When the posse arrives, combine them with your own men and join me out there. Who's in charge at the Parramatta Barracks?'

'First Lieutenant Bradbury, sir,' George replied, 'since Captain Macarthur's overseas.'

'Buying more sheep, no doubt? The first major uprising the colony's seen in sixteen years and the man's away on business. Anyway, I'm off without any further delay,' the governor added as he looked back at George and made for the front door. 'Follow me out as soon as the posse gets here.'

Back in the Barracks — officially known as 'The Governor's Domain' following the construction within it of a fine stone mansion overlooking the parade square — Daniel was considering his options. The only intelligence he had at this stage suggested that his best policy was to remain with the core of his trained troops within the Domain in order to beat off an anticipated attack by a mob of poorly armed, probably untrained and almost certainly badly led convicts. On the other hand, the people caught in lonely homesteads and isolated farms between Parramatta and Castle Hill were entitled to expect protection from a lawless group of desperate men released from bondage and looking for food, drink, weapons and vulnerable females. For the time being, he kept his men at the 'at ease' position, but still in their traditional square formation, while he tried to decide what, on balance, was the best course to pursue.

Shortly after midnight there was a commotion at the main gate and one of the posted sentinels yelled back into the parade square, 'Sir, there's a man here who claims to have come from the convict lot. Do you want him shot?'

'No!' Daniel replied. 'Send him in to see me at once, but keep your eyes on the road outside, in case he's a decoy.'

The man was escorted into the square and Daniel kept him at bayonet length in case he had instructions to assassinate whoever was in charge of the Barracks. He was dressed in what remained of a convict uniform and was sweaty and covered in dust and grime as he stood before Daniel, twisting his hands in a nervous gesture as he stared at the bayonet pointing at his gut.

'Who exactly *are* you and what do you want?' Daniel demanded.

The man swallowed hard, then succumbed to a dusty cough before asking for a drink of water. Daniel instructed one of his men to bring it out and the man thanked him profusely before downing it in one eager gulp, belching and explaining his business. 'Nathan Gridley, sir. A prisoner from the farm out there. Seven years fer burglary and assault, three years left ter serve. I were meant to travel out to Green Hills, out near the Hawkesbury, to tell the other lot that we were on, 'cos our signal fire don't seem to 'ave worked.'

'You're not making sense, Gridley,' Daniel told him with a frown. 'Start at the beginning. What's going on out at the farm?'

'All the prisoners've broken out, sir. The leader's that mad Irish bastard Cunningham, an' nobody 'ad the guts ter tell 'im where 'e got off. One've the other prisoners — a geezer called Cavanagh — set fire to one o' the 'uts in the camp. Because it's on a hill, Cunningham meant the blaze as a signal to other convict groups out west as far as the Hawkesbury, only it seems that they couldn't've seen it, 'cos nobody came. So I was sent ter round 'em up, only I came straight ter warn *you*, sir. I 'opes as 'ow yer'll put in a good word for me wi' the governor, an' maybe get me sentence reduced, 'cos if Cunningham finds out what I've done, 'e'll slit me throat as soon as look at me.'

'Where are Cunningham and his men now?' Daniel asked.

'On their way over 'ere, sir,' Gridley replied, the fear evident in his wide eyes. 'They was plannin' on stealin' guns an' suchlike from farms and the like on the way across, then marching back west to the Hawkesbury ter stage a mass rebellion. They reckon they can get a ship ter take 'em ter China.'

Daniel called a Corporal over from the men standing in the square watching the proceedings. 'Corporal Denning, take this man to the brig and make sure that he's fed, watered and guarded, for his own safety. Any attempt on his part to escape from the brig and you have my order to run him through with your bayonet. As for you, Mr. Gridley, if your information turns out to be correct, I'll be sure to let the governor know of your brave work tonight.'

The rebels led by Cunningham came upon them an hour later, running up the dusty road from the north-west. As the first of them dropped under a hail of musket fire from the compound fence, the rest scattered into the scrub, where they lay for some minutes before crawling away and reforming well out of musket range, in a surly crowd whose loud and arguing voices could be heard from the parade square. Then the arguing seemed to fizzle out after a few loud shouts and in the half light of a waning moon on a cloudy night the would-be attackers appeared to slink back to wherever they had come from.

Daniel stood his men down with instructions that they were to keep their weapons loaded, but to refresh themselves in the mess room and await further orders. He doubled the watch on the gate, supplementing, with rostered groups of his own men, the volunteers who were eager to rush out and suppress any possible attacks on the vulnerable properties that they had left unguarded and which in many cases contained their women and children. It was time to await reinforcements and further orders.

Daniel was leaning against the Commissary door, swallowing a lukewarm tin mug of tea laced with goats' milk, when he heard the thundering of hooves from the south-east, along the road that now linked Parramatta with Sydney, followed by a shouted challenge from the front gate. There was a responding yell from whoever was seeking access to the Domain and Daniel lurched to attention as he recognised the burly figure of Governor King and the black hats of his mounted escort, as they halted in the centre of the square and leaped from their saddles. Daniel yelled for grooms to tend to the horses in what passed for a stables block in what was essentially an infantry barracks, then stepped forward out of the gloom of the doorway and saluted.

'First Lieutenant Bradbury, sir. Acting Commandant of the Domain.'

Governor King snorted as he dusted down his tunic. 'I hope your men are better trained in fighting the enemy than they are at recognising their own governor,' he replied. 'Some oaf at the gate was offering to shoot at us.'

'In the main, they're only local volunteers, sir,' Daniel told him. 'My fulltime force are taking a refreshment break awaiting further orders.'

'A refreshment break?' Governor King thundered back. 'Why aren't they out there, suppressing this uprising?'

'Because, sir,' Daniel explained as diplomatically as he could, 'our first priority must be to guard your Domain and we don't have enough men to go scouring the countryside at dead of night.'

'You soon will have,' King replied. 'There's a full garrison from Sydney, plus a civilian posse, heading out behind us under the command of Major Johnston. I've brought Miles and Potter with me, as you can see.'

Daniel breathed a sigh of relief, then felt a pang of alarm when he realised that this would have left the women and children defenceless unless George had retained the presence of mind to leave men behind at Annandale. Putting the thought away for the moment, he offered to take the governor and his escort into the Mess for some refreshment.

'Might as well,' King replied, 'since Johnston and his lot are a good hour behind us.'

In fact, a pale March sunrise was appearing beyond the hills to the east before a weary force of almost a hundred men tramped up the dusty road, with George ahead of them on his horse, accompanied by a uniformed lieutenant from Sydney who Daniel had never met. Orders were yelled for the latest arrivals to be granted entry through the gate and Daniel hurried forward to greet George as he eased himself from the saddle with a muted oath.

'No wonder I opted for the marines. Thank God I wasn't posted to Cavalry — my arse feels like it's on fire.'

'Are the women and children OK?' Daniel asked with his heart in his mouth.

'Of course,' George assured him. 'Martha says to take care and to shoot the one responsible for Rebecca being woken after she'd just got her to sleep for the third time.'

'You left someone guarding them, I hope?'

George gave him the benefit of a disapproving look. 'That's why I'm a major, Lieutenant — I can think *and* scratch my balls at the same time. As for the Macarthur family down the road there, I've had them taken in that fancy wagon of theirs back to the Harbour, where they can take a ship to England if things go wrong out here. Now, tell me what's happening and why you're still in barracks. I take it that the governor arrived?'

'He's on his third mug of coffee,' Daniel replied, 'and he seems to be getting more uppity by the mug full. Wants to know why we're not out there fertilising his precious farm with convict blood and I'll give you the same answer I gave him — give me the men and I'll do the job.'

'Have you seen anything of the convicts?'

'They tried to attack the Domain during the night. They left a few dead in the Castle Hill road out there, then ran back from whence they came, as the Bible puts it.'

'On foot?'

'No sign of any horses that I could see, but there must be several hundred of them and I doubt if the entire colony has as many horses as that.'

'They can have this sorry nag,' George commented as he yelled for someone to take its bridle. 'Now then, lead me to the governor.'

They sat around the only serviceable table in the Officers' Mess, drinking coffee, munching on hot bread that the cook had been hauled out of bed to bake and debating tactics. George was particularly interested to learn that the leaders of the rebellion appeared to be Irish Catholics.

'You got any priests living locally?' he asked Daniel.

'There's Father Dixon here in the Domain,' Daniel responded. 'He's a lazy fat loafer most of the time and according to what I've heard his penances all take liquid form, but I suppose one cleric is as good as another.'

'I'd remind you, Lieutenant, that the Church of Rome is directly descended from St. Peter, who was our Lord's chosen vessel for the creation of the Christian faith,' King interrupted and Daniel reddened slightly before George came to his rescue.

'Forgive my lieutenant if he seemed somewhat irreverent just then, Governor, but my point is that we would be wise to take with us, when we seek to parley with these Irish peasants, someone whose authority they respect, since they clearly don't respect ours.'

'Good point,' King conceded. 'How many men will you take with you and when exactly did you propose to stop drinking this dreadful coffee and get out and restore some sort of military authority over the surrounding countryside?'

George deliberately refilled his mug from the pot before replying. 'It's probably as long since I walked twenty odd miles at the double march as it is since *you* did, Governor, but I think we may reasonably conclude that the Sydney troops at our command are right now nursing sore feet and examining their boots for holes. They clearly need a good rest before we can order them back onto their feet, but what I propose is that I ride ahead with Lieutenant Miles and offer the rebels surrender terms.'

'*Surrender?*' King bellowed. 'These men are in armed rebellion against my authority and you suggest that we offer them surrender terms?'

'If we can persuade them to surrender,' George argued coolly and levelly, 'we won't be risking the lives of any of our men. The uprising will be over, law and order will have been restored and our point will have been made that we still run the colony.'

King glared at Daniel. 'Do you share this madness with your Major?' he demanded.

Daniel looked him firmly in the eye as he replied, 'I follow the Major's orders, sir.'

The governor looked round for support from the two officers who had ridden out to Parramatta with him, both of whom sheepishly agreed that surrender without loss of men was a positive outcome, if it could be achieved. King conceded the point with bad grace and asked what use George intended to make of those soldiers who had spent the night in the security of the Domain.

'I propose,' George replied, 'that Lieutenant Bradbury here takes his men to Castle Hill, in order to assess the damage and restore our authority.'

King nodded his assent and the matter was settled without Daniel even being consulted. What he discovered, when he and a dozen armed troopers breasted the rise and surveyed the remains of the governor's highly-prized Government Farm, was a tangled collection of demolished and still smouldering convict huts, a dead convict guard lying in a congealed, fly-plagued welter of his own blood, a Commissary hut empty of anything that might be of use to a fighting man on the march and several dead cattle and sheep, lying where they had fallen after their throats had been cut.

They then set about the dismal process of checking with outlying farmstead owners regarding the fates that had befallen them once the convicts had broken loose. Scores of men had been obliged, out of fear for their lives, or those of their loved ones, to join the power-crazed mob, while scores of their womenfolk told, through the blank, shattered set of their eyes, how they had fared at the hands of beasts who had been without women until unleashed into the surrounding countryside with all the moral authority with which possession of an axe or knife could imbue them.

Daniel was sickened by it all and, leaving the men who had ridden out with him to make what effort they could to restore normality, he rode slowly and alone back to the Domain, trying to imagine how he could have survived with his sanity intact if those at the mercy of the convicts had been his own wife and family.

George rode with Lieutenant Miles and caught up with the rebel horde on its way back towards Constitution Hill. There were still several hundred of them and they laughed and jeered as they watched George and Lieutenant Miles approach slowly on horseback, accompanied by a fat priest on a donkey who appeared to be attempting to recreate Christ's entry into Jerusalem on Palm Sunday.

Miles was sent forward first and he asked to speak to their leader. A surly looking man still dressed in his convict garb stepped forward from the group at the foot of the hill and answered the question.

'I'm Phil Cunningham and these men are the new army of the recently created Free Irish Republic of New South Wales. Who might *you* be, soldier boy?'

'William Miles, lieutenant in the New South Wales Corps, acting as envoy for my commanding officer Major George Johnston.'

'And what does Major Johnston command of *us*, bearing in mind that we outnumber you, on my count, by some one hundred to one?'

'Your peaceful surrender,' Miles demanded, his head held high.

Cunningham burst out laughing. 'You amuse me, soldier boy, so I will not have your head torn from your body. Return to your Major and tell him from the President of the Free Irish Republic of New South Wales to stick his surrender terms up his arse.'

Miles turned his mount and rode sedately back to where George and Father Dixon sat awaiting his return.

'Well?' George demanded.

'He declined our offer, sir,' Miles replied diplomatically.

'Well, we *did* offer,' George responded with a grin. 'Go back down the road and don't reappear up it again until you have the combined foot brigades with you. Then line them up here and await further orders.'

Miles nodded and rode off back down the track. He returned with the foot contingent half an hour later, and George urged his horse forward and reined it in where Miles had been parleying earlier with Cunningham, who had now been joined by fellow conspirators and was grinning wildly.

'Decided that your arse isn't big enough to shove your surrender terms up it, have you?' he crowed.

George smiled back pleasantly. 'I see that you have retained all the manners that your bog-infected whore of a mother bequeathed you, so I won't seek to engage you in civilised conversation regarding the immediate futures of your syphilitic bodies. But you might wish to consider the state of your souls. As you can see, I have a priest with me and he seeks the opportunity to offer you God's grace and comfort before you launch yourselves into the fires of Hell.'

'Go to Hell yourself!' Cunningham roared back.

George shrugged. 'As you can see, the numbers have now been re-balanced and by my calculation at least fifty of you will drop with musket balls in your chests on my giving one simple command. You may play dice with your own souls, if you wish, but what about the others you have misled to this point in their lives?'

'And if we surrender?' asked the man standing next to Cunningham, speaking for the first time.

'Then there will be no need for anyone to shoot,' George told him.

Cunningham appeared to be about to make another rude response, but the other man grabbed his arm.

'He has a point, my friend. We're outgunned and if we walk away from this now, there'll be other opportunities, surely?'

'You'd trust the word of an English bastard?' Cunningham demanded.

'No,' his companion replied, 'but I'd trust the word of a priest.' He nodded towards Father Dixon, who so far had said nothing.

Cunningham thought for a moment, then nodded grudgingly and withdrew a pistol from inside his shirt, which he handed up to George. The other man took a similar weapon from his jacket and threw it onto the dusty ground.

George and Lieutenant Miles dismounted, drew their pistols from their tunics, held them up at the heads of the two surrendering rebels and advised them that they were under military arrest. Then George turned a blind eye and walked away as the men from Sydney opened fire on the surrendered convicts. By the time that George had persuaded them to cease their firing, half of them were dead, and the remaining half were only too happy to surrender.

The footsore prisoners were marched into the Domain and handed over to others to await their fates. After a hearty dinner, the officers drew up the lists and nine of them were hanged that same afternoon. A party was sent out to the Prospect road with a corpse and a gibbet to remind every passing traveller of the military superiority of the governor of New South Wales and to Daniel fell the stomach-churning duty of overseeing the many floggings that took place as the sun began to set on one of the worst days of his life. Two of them were ordered to undergo as many lashes as they could survive without any danger to their lives and towards the end Daniel was obliged to duck behind a store shed in order to vomit.

It was a silent and surly Daniel who rode alongside George on his return to Annandale the following morning. Lieutenant Miles had obligingly agreed to supervise the Domain Barracks in return for the opportunity to occupy Daniel's quarters in the company of a convict kitchen hand whose promiscuity was legendary throughout the regiment, and Daniel had two whole days off.

The women came to the door of the Annandale house, the children at their side, as they heard the horses approach. George dismounted first and was eagerly grabbed by Esther and hugged around the neck. Martha was clearly waiting to do something similar, but as Daniel dismounted and looked across at his beautiful wife, his helpless young son with a toy in his hand and tiny Rebecca rubbing the sleep from her eyes, he felt his legs refuse to move further. He could see Martha staring at him in curiosity mingled with apprehension and he simply shook his head silently.

She ran across the narrow lawn and crushed him to her as the tears rolled down his face and he clung to her like a life raft. 'Please don't make me go back there, darling. In the name of God, if you love me, don't make me be a soldier anymore!'

18

Martha cradled Daniel in her arms until he finally fell asleep and murmured reassuringly to him when he woke three times from a fitful slumber to cry out in alarm and despair. She slipped out of bed just as day broke the following morning and sat on the front veranda until Esther appeared as usual to supervise her children's breakfast. Esther sat down beside her and handed her a mug of tea, then put her arm across Martha's shoulders.

'What happened to Daniel out there?' she asked.

Martha shook her head. 'He won't say, but whatever it was it's devastated him. I don't think it's fear — he's too brave for that — but I think it's connected with what he was forced to watch.'

'Do you think he'll resign his commission?'

'I sincerely hope he *does*, if that's what's eating into his soul. But if I know my man as well as I hope I do, he won't be prepared to face the accusation of cowardice.'

'Martha, dear,' Esther assured her, 'no one who witnessed how he faced up to those natives could ever accuse him of cowardice, least of all George.'

Martha looked across at her close friend with pleading eyes. 'I think George may be the key to all this. If he could only persuade Daniel that there'd be no dishonour in resigning his commission, all might be well.'

Esther nodded in agreement and gazed across the lawn, to where uniformed marines were beginning to emerge from the accommodation hut in order to replace the night watch. 'What do you think he could do instead?' she asked.

Martha shook her head in uncertainty. 'I've lain awake half the night wondering about that. From what he's told me, his only other experience was in a tobacco enterprise in Bristol — perhaps we could start growing tobacco or something.'

Just then, George walked out chewing on a piece of bread and watching his men assemble for the morning roster. It fell silent and as he looked down at the two women seated near the front door he spoke softly. 'I heard you talking about Daniel — I think he's had it with the marines, but I've been thinking. Is he up to talking, Martha?'

'He certainly did a lot of it in his sleep last night, but I'm not sure that he'll be quite prepared yet to discuss his problem with his commanding officer.'

'Then we have to hope that he's prepared to do so with a friend,' George replied as he walked past them, across the lawn and down towards his hut.

Matthew appeared at the front door, demanding his breakfast, and Martha realised that it wouldn't be long before Rebecca made the same demand and would probably leave her room in order to wake Daniel to do so. Martha followed Esther inside and into their main bedroom. She looked down at the bed and saw that Daniel's eyes were open and fixed on the ceiling. He looked across at her and smiled thinly.

'Sorry for over-sleeping. We should be making the best of every hour I'm home and here I am, wasting the first day out of two.'

Checking that Rebecca was still in the land of infant dreams, Martha sat on the side of the bed next to Daniel, stroked his forehead and then leaned down to kiss him. 'Does it have to be only two days?' she asked.

Daniel frowned. 'Don't tempt me, sweetheart. I can't leave poor old Miles out there for more than the two days he generously offered to cover for me, but perhaps you might have a word with Esther, who's George's real commanding officer, and then he might be persuaded to extend my leave and send someone else out there.'

'How about making that leave permanent?' Martha suggested.

Daniel slid from under the sheets and searched the bedroom floor for the uniform breeches he'd discarded the night before. Martha watched him for a moment, then giggled. 'If men weren't so eager to drop their trousers in the company of a woman, they might remember where they'd left them when they come round the next morning. They're in the laundry basket, since you don't need them today. I've put your smart brown civilian ones over the chair in the corner.'

'Where would I be without you?' Daniel said.

'Without me, you'd be going back to something you've obviously grown to hate. But *with* me, there's hope that you'll find your true role in life.'

Daniel looked back at her with a puzzled expression. 'It's too early in the morning for riddles and guessing games. What are you getting at?'

'Come and have some breakfast and I'll tell you.'

'Would you like eggs this morning?' the housekeeper Sarah asked when Daniel had sat down at the table. 'That old broiler finally realised what God put her into this life for and I got three from underneath her before she pecked me half to death.'

Daniel shook his head. 'No thanks, Sarah — just some bread and some of that lovely cumquat jam of yours, if George hasn't scoffed the lot. And perhaps some more tea — I think it could be a three mug morning.'

'They say that over twenty of those escaped convicts were shot dead,' Sarah prattled breezily as she attacked the loaf with a bread knife, her back to the table. 'Do you by any chance know if one of them was a Michael Flynn? I got right friendly with him when he was on the hospital detail.'

Daniel's face froze in the horror of the remembrance and Martha got up quickly from the breakfast table and took the knife from Sarah's hand.

'I'll see to the breakfast, Sarah,' she assured her. 'There's some washing in our laundry basket, if you'd be so good.'

Sarah left the kitchen with a puzzled frown, wondering if perhaps she'd inadvertently said the wrong thing, and in the awkward silence Martha continued slicing bread as if she had a regiment to feed. Eventually it was Daniel who broke the silence.

'We can't simply not talk about it. After all, it was George who let it happen.'

'And George who has to answer for it in his conscience,' Martha reminded him. 'But if you're only going to be home for two days, can we not find something more cheerful to talk about?'

'It wasn't the shootings anyway,' Daniel persisted. 'I didn't have to watch that, thank God. But if you'd been forced to stand and watch the floggings afterwards...'

'Don't!' Martha said. 'And that's an order — from *your* commanding officer. And from the woman you married, the woman you hopefully still love, and the woman who wants her man to be happy when he's home.'

'Home,' Daniel repeated in a distant, reflective, tone. 'How I wish to God this *were* my real home and not some sort of pleasure palace that I visit on leave.'

'Couldn't you get a transfer?'

'I'm sure George would be able to wangle something, but I'm afraid it's gone beyond that. This regime is evil, Martha — the strong brutalising the weak, the fortunate ruling the lives of the unfortunate. Surely I don't have to explain that to you, given the circumstances in which we first met?'

She slid into the chair next to his, all thought of cutting bread abandoned. 'But it won't always be like this, will it? According to what George tells us over supper every evening, this new governor he works for wants to build a new society out here and then surely it won't just be a matter of convicts being guarded by marines? Every new arrival brings a boatload of free settlers, determined to start a new life where here's no class distinction.'

'And every new boat brings us a fresh supply of convicts,' Daniel reminded her. 'The Corps is recruiting more men daily and Rebecca will be a married woman with children of her own before the governor realises his empty dream. The present reality is hangings and floggings.'

Martha's hand slid gently over his, as she looked up into his eyes. 'I want you here every day, Daniel. And so do Matthew and Rebecca. If you disapprove so strongly of what you're being forced to do, why don't you do something else?'

'Like what, exactly?' Daniel laughed ironically. 'I'm only fit for brutalising my fellow human beings, and now it seems that I don't have the stomach for even that.'

'Your life before you became a soldier — weren't you in some sort of commerce and can't you use that experience out here? They tell me the governor's desperate to establish a real society out here, like the one in London, and surely there'd be a place in it for someone like you?'

Daniel laughed again. 'In commerce, you need contacts — "patrons", if you like. The only people I know out here are soldiers and here I am dreaming of leaving the only sort of society I really know. None of those could give me a commercial opening, could they? And in any case, I only know the tobacco trade — we don't have one out here, as far as I'm aware. We don't even smoke the stuff ourselves, apart from George and that dreadful pipe of his.'

'Leave that side of things to me,' Martha replied with the glint of battle in her eye. 'Right now, your first priority must be getting out of the army.'

At that moment Matthew appeared in the kitchen doorway, complaining of a sore tummy and Martha hustled him back out with a stern warning that if this was another of his ploys to avoid being available when the childrens' tutor arrived for the day, he'd be in serious trouble. Daniel smiled, remembering his own childhood strategies to avoid the village school and found himself reflecting on the conversation he'd just had with Martha. Perhaps if he'd paid more attention to his studies, he might now be in a position to offer the colony something other than bayonet and noose. He shuddered again at the memory of Parramatta and wandered outside.

George appeared by his side as he sat on the veranda sipping tea and munching on dry bread. Both men gazed silently across at the uniformed men lounging around their hut and talking idly, before George voiced his thoughts. 'Maybe one day we'll make something of them, but it'll take a miracle to create an officer between them.'

Daniel sighed. 'Is this your less than subtle introduction into a conversation about me bottling it yesterday?'

'Do you *want* to talk about it?' George asked.

'No.'

'Well I do. I have to make a full report to old Pompous Pants today and I need your input on how the reprisals went.'

Daniel swallowed hard, then let fly. 'It was the most disgusting thing I've ever had the misfortune to witness, George. Grown men reduced to strips of bleeding flesh and screaming to God for mercy. Is that what our governor calls "reprisals", because if so I'd be delighted to let him supervise the next flogging he orders. Right now, if I could throw my commission into the creek at the back there, I'd happily do so. What's the going rate for cowardice? Court martial, followed by dishonourable discharge? Put my name down for one of each when you go across the water this morning.'

George took the seat next to Daniel's and relit his pipe — a common tactic of his when taking time to think. 'I've been in the service for damned near twenty years and I've learned to judge men by all sorts of standards, including their courage. The sort of courage required when you're facing a line of enemy muskets is one thing, but the courage to sit alone on a beach with the enemy at your back, armed with spears, in the hope of earning their friendship, is another kind of courage altogether. Don't call yourself a coward, Daniel, just because you have the humanity to shrink from the pain of others.'

'How have you managed to stand it all these years?' Daniel asked. 'I can't carry on as a marine, after yesterday — I just *can't*.'

George rested a consoling hand on his shoulder. 'You won't be going back to Rose Hill, you can be assured of that. Bill Miles may be a good soldier, but he's bloody dreadful at paperwork and the governor's forever bending my ear to replace him with someone who can tell the difference between an urgent despatch and a goat's arse. From what the men were telling me on the way home, he's as happy as a pig in muck being shacked up with a doxy who bangs like a barn door in a howling gale, so he can stay where he is and you can join me at the Governor's Mansion, reassuring the old misery that he still retains full control of his colony.'

'And how long will *that* last?' Daniel asked suspiciously. 'I've been in the service long enough to know that duties have to be rotated regularly.'

'Not once you're working for the governor they don't,' George reassured him. 'If he's happy with your work, he'll hang on to you like a drowning man to a lifebuoy. For long enough for you to resign your commission and get a real job, anyway.'

'And what sort of job would that be?'

George nodded towards the paddock between the garden fence and the creek, in which a fine herd of plump cattle were grazing contentedly on rich pasture. 'I've got nearly two hundred head of Herefords out there and while they feed themselves, they don't *sell* themselves. I've been thinking for some time of employing someone to search out markets in England, or maybe the Cape. But I know about as much about marketing cattle as I do about playing the piano, whereas *you* — or so your wife tells me — have been known to sell tobacco.'

Daniel smiled to himself. Martha had clearly wasted no time. But it surely wasn't going to be that simple. 'Presumably you couldn't afford to pay me a first lieutenant's salary?'

'Of course not. You'd be selling cattle, not gold. But I'm probably not the only one in need of sales assistance. Macarthur's expected back shortly — he's got even more problems in that department than I have, or so his dreadful harpy of a wife was bleating on about the last time she cursed us with her company. No doubt he could employ your talents as well.'

Daniel spent a few moments in thought. He reminded himself that it was the only immediate way of avoiding a return to Parramatta and that Martha would not thank him for throwing away her first lifeline. 'Very well, George,' he agreed. 'The day after tomorrow I'll join you in the cutter and do my best to impress the governor in my new duties and then in a few weeks I'll resign my commission and live on half-pay enjoying your charitable hospitality here in Annandale.'

'You got that half right at least,' George confirmed. 'You start tomorrow trying to make sense of my sales records in the office in the back room of where you'll be living as part of your remuneration as my Sales Manager. As for the governor, you won't be renewing your acquaintance with him until after the week's leave that I just granted you.'

A week to the day later, Daniel looked out beyond the bow of the cutter, as it made its way across the harbour, at a Sydney he barely recognised. Where there had once been huts there were now brick buildings, in between which lines of convicts were hammering wooden cobbles into the earth in order to improve the road quality under the hooves of horses and the wheels of coaches and wagons. There was a governor's Domain here, as well as the one at Parramatta and the governor's coach was drawn up ready for their arrival at the quayside. Uniformed men saluted them in the doorway to the mansion and their boots almost glided down the highly polished floorboards as George ushered Daniel to his desk in the Aide's Room, as it was called, upon which piles of documents awaited his attention.

'Leave all that for the moment,' George instructed him, 'and come and reassure our illustrious governor that his correspondence is now in the hands of someone whose reading and writing skills were not confined to the race track.'

Governor King sniffed when he recognised Daniel, but gestured them both into seats in front of his long mahogany desk. 'The last time we met, Lieutenant, you were apologising for the quality of the coffee out at Rose Hill Barracks and assuring me that you simply follow Major Johnston's orders. But they were well carried out, from what I've been informed. Thank you for your graphic account of the hangings and floggings, by the way. A job well done.'

George placed a restraining hand on Daniel's arm as the latter turned white with fury and grabbed the conversation before the silence could prove too inviting for his hot-headed subordinate. 'Lieutenant Bradbury here will be replacing Lieutenant Miles, in response to your request to have someone available who understands the mysteries of the English language. He'll be residing at Annandale for the time being, but a land grant of his own might make it easier for him to perform his duties.'

While Daniel raised his eyebrows in mute surprise, King got up and walked to the side wall, where he studied a map of the area for a moment before responding.

'We could do with filling up that area to the west of your estate, Major,' he observed. 'At present it's just a useless wasteland between one of the bays and the Parramatta Road and it would be good to have a marine officer settled there, to add to our security.'

And to add to the insecurity of the family that lives there, Daniel thought, but remained silent.

King continued, 'Five acres, from the foreshore to the road — take your pick of which five, then talk to the Surveyor-

General and have him mark out the plot and arrange the conveyance.'

'Thank you, sir,' Daniel said.

'Think nothing of it,' King replied. 'It's only in order that you may carry out your duties more efficiently. And you'll soon be earning that land, trust me — Lieutenant Miles left his desk looking like a dog's breakfast.'

Three weeks later, by which time Daniel had finally got his head around the procedural protocols within the governor's office and was meeting regularly with George to arrange the disposition of Corps 'troopers', as they were now called, he and Martha were standing at the top of a small rise looking down at one of the harbour's many inlets. Before them was a field of scrub and some distance behind them the road to Parramatta that was in effect the extension to the road that had once led to the brickworks and had run past their first hut. Sarah was back at Annandale with the children and they held hands like first-time sweethearts, taking in the sun's rays bouncing off the calm water below them and imagining rolling lawns and ornamental gardens.

'This is obviously the best place for the house,' Martha announced. 'We can sit on the front veranda of an evening and gaze at the water while we sip elderflower champagne and watch the children playing on the lawns.'

Daniel frowned slightly. 'I think you'll find that this view will be from the *back* of the house, strictly speaking. Since the road is back there behind us, the obvious front of the house will face the road. The governor's very graciously offered to sell me one of his carriages — the one with the canvas roof. It's not very grand, but it only needs one horse to pull it and I'm getting a sore bottom from riding a saddle to work and back every day. I can just imagine a sweeping approach to the front door and the kids running out to meet me when I come home every evening.'

'Will you be able to use convict labour?' she asked.

Daniel smiled. 'There have to be *some* advantages in putting up with the governor's pompous prattle every day. He's left convict allocations to me, so what do *you* think?'

'When do they start and when can we move in? And will Matthew get his own tutor, or will he have to travel down the road to George's place every day?'

'Too many questions all at once,' Daniel chided her gently as he kissed the tip of her nose. 'We haven't even given the place a name yet. Any ideas?'

'How about "Bradbury House"?'

'That doesn't really do justice to the land as a whole. We need a name like the one George chose for Annandale, where he was born. I grew up in a sleepy village south of Bristol called "Ridley Magna", which doesn't quite sound right for a New South Wales park. Where did you grow up? Somewhere in Wiltshire, wasn't it?'

'Trowbridge, although I was actually born in my mother's parents' house in a village called Haberfield. It was only a church, an inn and a big house in its own grounds and it became part of Yarnbrook when my grandparents died and the estate was sold to a dairy farmer. But "Haberfield" would do, unless you have any better ideas.'

'Welcome to Haberfield,' Daniel replied, as he squeezed her waist tightly.

19

In July 1805, the colony welcomed back John Macarthur, whose cabin bag was stuffed with export contracts for pure Merino lambs' wool drawn up by lawyers acting for merchants in Manchester and Liverpool. George appeared in the doorway of Daniel's office two days after the anchoring of the *Argo* and peered in. Assuring himself that Daniel was alone in his office, and having doubled-checked behind him that the corridor was empty, he sidled in and took the chair in front of Daniel's desk.

'Have you had a chance to open all the despatches from London?'

'Some of them,' Daniel replied. 'Did you have one in particular in mind?'

'There must be something there from the Army Office,' George said in a low conspiratorial voice. 'I got one advising me that Macarthur's resigned his commission and that I need a new captain.'

'Well don't look at me,' Daniel replied. 'I'll be handing in my ticket any time now. What's the problem?'

'I just can't imagine the old rogue waving goodbye to a captain's stipend unless he was either very sure of his sheep business, or he was forced into it. His old crow of a wife's putting it around that he was offered another five thousand acres in return for his valiant work out here in the colony, which as we both know consisted largely of shearing woolly arses, and Esther wants me to find out the truth, so that she can ruin the next dinner party by announcing it over the candles.'

Daniel grinned. 'Remind me never to get on the wrong side of your wife. In the meantime, there's a court martial despatch bag on your side of the desk. If you choose to open it, I can hardly prevent my commanding officer supervising my work.'

George broke the seals gleefully, then rustled through half a dozen copied reports of courts martial held in London during the previous year until he found the one he was looking for and let out a joyful chuckle. 'Here it is! He was apprehended in London for dereliction of duty, but escaped a court martial because, according to him, the slack way in which the colony was being run by the governor made it impossible for him to perform his duties as an officer of His Majesty's forces. The Judge-Advocate announced that, and I quote, "for the sake of harmony within this vital colony, any alleged irregularity on the part of the prisoner will not be investigated further, until such time as His Majesty's Secretary of State for the Colonies can investigate other divers complaints regarding the administration of the Colony of New South Wales." What does all that mean in English?'

Daniel leaned forward and lowered his voice. 'Yesterday, the governor got me to draft a request from him for leave of absence while a wholesale enquiry was undertaken regarding his running of the colony. He's been advised in previous despatches that letters of complaint have been travelling back to London by almost every departing vessel regarding how he's conducting himself out here. He's hopping mad and believes that someone is co-ordinating the whole thing at this end.'

George tapped his nose in the time-honoured gesture of secrecy and whispered back, 'My money's on Elizabeth Macarthur. She's forever complaining that John isn't getting the support and recognition that he deserves. I think she fancies herself as the governor's wife.'

'God help us if she succeeds,' Daniel groaned.

'That brings me to the bad news,' George added. 'Elizabeth's organising a homecoming supper to celebrate John's safe return and we're all commanded to attend. Esther will never forgive Martha if she ducks out of it, leaving Esther at the mercy of the old bag's snobby tongue and if Martha *does* duck out of it, I'll never forgive *you*.'

Daniel groaned. 'When is it?'

'Saturday evening. And it's best bib and tucker.'

The appointed day came only too quickly and Daniel braced himself for the usual catty exchanges across the dinner table as the former convict servants served dish after elegant dish. But to his surprise Elizabeth Macarthur seemed too distracted by some other matter to engage in her usual loud proclamations of John's estimation within the community, and the correspondingly humbler achievements of others. However, Daniel winced and glanced quickly at Esther's frosty expression as Elizabeth launched into a hand-waving description of the additional acreage that John had been granted 'from the hand of the Colonial Secretary himself', to which the entire family would soon be transferring and for which they had already chosen the name 'Camden Park', in honour of the Marquess of Camden, Secretary of State for the Colonies, who had granted them the land. It lay half a day's ride from Annandale and George's other property at Bankstown lay between the two, with Elizabeth Farm, where they were enjoying supper that evening, to the north-west and as close to Parramatta as Daniel felt comfortable travelling.

As the coffee was served, Elizabeth rose to her feet and announced, 'We'll leave the men to discuss their exciting new business project, while we ladies withdraw to the drawing room to consider another momentous matter that has been left in my experienced hands by none other than the Marquess himself.'

As they swept out like a squadron of new-born chicks being led to the water by an old mother hen, Daniel poured himself a glass of port from the circulating decanter and awaited further revelations regarding the 'exciting new business project' that Elizabeth had foreshadowed in her departing remarks. He looked back up from the glass and was somewhat taken aback to see John Macarthur staring thoughtfully at him across the table.

'Daniel, how much law do you know?'

'Very little, in truth,' Daniel admitted. 'My older brother Joseph is the lawyer in the family, why?'

'Do you want to explain, George?' Macarthur said.

George looked back down the table at Daniel. 'I gather that you once imported tobacco from Virginia to Bristol?'

'Correct,' Daniel confirmed.

'What do you know about something called "charterparties?" Have I got the term right?'

'Charterparties, certainly,' Daniel agreed. 'They're contracts for the loading of a ship with a cargo. I was involved with them all the time. But that was years ago, and you still haven't answered my question. Why is the extent of my legal knowledge suddenly important?'

George looked across at John Macarthur, who picked up the thread.

'As you probably know from your duties in the governor's office — and please don't feel obliged to politely deny it — the governor and I don't exactly see eye to eye on the direction in which this colony should be heading. For some years now the economic development of New South Wales has hung on the export of my sheep and wool — and to a certain extent George's cattle — to England. I came back with some important ongoing export contracts for fleeces into Manchester via the Port of Liverpool and I'm only a short step away from being able to export cattle carcases into the Port of London. All I need are the ships, and the governor thinks he can spike my guns by denying me access to empty holds on government ships heading back home. But he can't stop me using my own ships and that's where you come in, Daniel.'

'How exactly?' Daniel asked, still bemused.

'By chartering the ships for us — George and I, that is. You're already doing that in a small way, with the cattle from Annandale that you've been organising onto government vessels going back via the Cape. We want you to charter your own ships, bring them out here, load them with our produce and send them back to London and Liverpool.'

'Chartering a ship is an awesome commercial risk,' Daniel pointed out.

'One has to speculate in order to accumulate,' Macarthur replied pompously, 'and we don't lack the finance, thanks to my first few successful cargoes. George and I will be going into partnership shortly and we wish to employ you on a full-time basis organising the ocean transport. George assures me that you're planning on handing in your ticket and we're within days of signing a lease on the old Commissary Store building, which the government no longer requires. However, if the governor finds out who the intending tenants are, he'll refuse to sign the lease. Perhaps your good lady could be prevailed upon once again to dust off her acting skills and pose as a newly-arrived free settler with trading ambitions. That's just the sort of initiative the governor approves of, provided that it has nothing to do with me.'

'I'm sure she'd be delighted,' Daniel replied, 'and I'll leave it to her to decide what business she's going to pretend to be in. Then you want me to set up some sort of shipping office, have I got it right?'

'Exactly right,' Macarthur confirmed. 'But you haven't asked about what's in it for you — that's always a good sign in an employee.'

'What's in it for me is a real job after I hand in my ticket,' Daniel replied, almost laughing with schoolboy enthusiasm at the way things were working out — thanks, no doubt, to a beautiful lady who not only shared his bed, but organised his very existence. 'I wasn't really looking forward to forfeiting a first lieutenant's pay.'

'But I'm afraid you'll have to,' George replied teasingly, enjoying the look of confusion that crossed Daniel's face. 'However, you'll presumably enjoy the promotion. We propose that your salary be pegged with that of a captain of marines. As it goes up, so does yours. If we start to make an absolute killing, we'll obviously slip you more. Are you with us?'

'You bet your life I am!' Daniel stood up and shook both men's hands enthusiastically. 'I'll hand in my ticket on Monday and if my information's correct I can start working for you full-time a month after that.'

He gave Martha the good news as soon as the ladies rejoined them, but was a little nonplussed by the fact that although she hugged and kissed him and made every delighted noise appropriate for a wife happy with her husband's change of fortune, it was as if she already knew. He put it down to the fact that she'd obviously been working behind the scenes for some time to ensure his honourable resignation from the working life he hated, and it wasn't until she climbed into bed beside him back at Annandale several hours later that he remembered something.

'What was the "momentous matter" that Elizabeth mentioned?'

'None of your business, darling, but it'll fit perfectly with acquiring the lease on the old Commissary Store.'

'Wives shouldn't keep secrets from their husbands.'

'That right? Well, I'll share a secret with you right now. I'm three months gone.'

Daniel marvelled at how life could turn around so favourably in such a short time and gave thanks to God and the mother who'd brought him into such a wonderful life.

20

Daniel smiled to himself as he signed the discharge document for the latest delivery and handed it back to the mariner who had accompanied the consignment note from the captain's cabin on board the *Parramatta*, all the way to the warehouse and head office of the Sydney English Exchange Institute at the far end of the newly-named High Street. On the main floor below Daniel's office, hired labourers were busily engaged in unloading barrels and boxes of goods as varied as fine French brandy and ornate candle-holders from Birmingham. There were ropes, gentlemen's hats, oil paintings, novels, bags of first-grade English flour, pewter mugs, bibles, perambulators and porcelain ornaments, all destined for the various merchants' stores further down the street, at a fat profit on resale to the partners of the Institute, of which he was now one.

But the most important cargoes would be the ones loaded onto the lower decks of the returning vessel after its short trip across the bay and into the Parramatta River. At the quay originally commissioned by a former governor it would take on board the latest fine fleeces from Elizabeth Farm and the live beasts from Camden, before slipping back to a more recent harbour to take on the latest carcasses from Annandale, which would be packed in ice from the ice-house at the bottom of the sloping ground at Haberfield. With a fair wind, the *Parramatta* would unload at Rotherhithe in time for the Christmas wholesale trade at London's Smithfield, before sailing north to Liverpool to offload bales of fleece and reload with the latest consignments eagerly awaited by Sydney merchants.

And all this was going on under the nose of the governor who, from his fine mansion in the 'Domain' at the other end the street, still kept up the appearance of running the colony, even though the real power had for some time been in the hands of the leading landholders who were the partners in the Institute, one of whom still notionally undertook the military duties that he now left largely to his subordinates.

It was less than a year since Governor King, under pressure from London to promote trade between the two capitals of London and Sydney, had conceded Macarthur's right to farm the massive 'cow pastures' holding out at Camden that he had been granted by the Colonial Secretary, pending a full-scale enquiry in Whitehall into the legality of the grant that seemed destined never to take place.

Shortly thereafter, he had granted audience to two ladies, one of whom, bearing a letter of introduction from Sir Joseph Banks, had successfully requested a fifty-year lease of the old Commissary Store. He had believed himself to be negotiating with a Mrs. Margery Moncrieff of Edinburgh, newly arrived to promote further trade links between 'the old country' and Sydney and was not to know that with the liberal application of sufficient quantities of make-up and suitable city gowns borrowed from Elizabeth Macarthur, Martha Bradbury could pass for twenty years older than she really was, while 'Esther Julian', her 'cousin' and 'colonial contact', was on hand to remind the governor that 'Mrs. Moncrieff' was highly connected in the London government circles in which Governor King's ongoing fitness to manage the colony was currently being debated.

'It was a shame to take the money,' Martha had told the assembled company in the newly-completed Haberfield house in which she had given birth to Mark Bradbury only weeks before adopting her Scottish persona and heading off to meet with the governor. Any possibility of the Bradbury brood outnumbering their Johnston neighbours had been convincingly forestalled by the birth of Maria, Esther's fifth daughter, a month after the pivotal meeting with the governor. A fourth daughter, Isabella, had just graduated from the nursery aged two, to join her three-year-old sister Blanche and the second oldest daughter, five-year-old Julia, in their romps up and down the lawns at Annandale, under the watchful gaze of George's marine detachment at the bottom of the garden and the ageing Sarah Biddle from her chair on the veranda. Sarah was now assisted by a second children's nurse, Lucy Bracegirdle, the daughter of emancipated convict Amos Bracegirdle and the object of marital ambitions on the part of family coachman Edward Tolhurst.

The oldest Johnston son, George Junior, now a tall sixteen year old, regularly rode around the cow pastures with his father, followed dutifully by his fourteen-year-old brother Robert, while seven-year-old David was already demonstrating a preference for books. The oldest child of the family, eighteen-year-old Roseanna, was tall and elegant, with a poise and dignity that belied the fact that she had been born in Newgate Gaol and suckled at her mother's breast in the foetid darkness below decks on the *Lady Penrhyn*. Her origins would no doubt one day come as a very pleasant surprise to her latest suitor, Isaac Nichols, himself an emancipated convict who in his darker moments felt himself beneath the ladylike object of his affections.

Daniel's rapid promotion to a partnership in the Institute that was a cheekily transparent 'cover' for the livestock- and fleece-trading activities of George and Macarthur was thanks to the generosity of his older brother Joseph. In one of his infrequent letters several Christmases ago, Joseph had advised Daniel that he had given up full-time legal practice and was now installed as a Fellow of Balliol College, Oxford, teaching undergraduates. Daniel had contacted him with a request for books and learned papers on those areas of English law in which he urgently required tuition and he was now something of a colonial expert on matters as varied as 'charterparties', 'salvage' and the curiously-named 'bonds of bottomry' that he hoped never to have to draft. On the commercial side, he knew the difference between bills of lading quoted 'free on board' and those subject to 'carriage, insurance and freight' and had ensured that sufficient goods came into Sydney in otherwise empty holds to justify the open myth that the Institute was importing valuable items of cultural and commercial significance, when in fact its primary income came from the export of fleece, live lambs and dead cattle.

The acquisition of the *Parramatta* had been a natural development, once Daniel had convinced George and John that they could increase their profits by a percentage in double figures by employing their own captain and crew on a return voyage basis and carrying their own produce in their own hold, rather than relying on the availability and goodwill of a potentially untrustworthy shipowner and his scrofulous crew. It had been this particular piece of inspired forward-thinking that had finally secured Daniel his partnership and his first annual bonus had ensured that the house at Haberfield, completed in time for Christmas 1805, wanted for nothing in the way of soft furnishings, wall hangings and other signs of middle-class affluence.

'Mrs. Bradbury to see you, sir,' his floor manager, James Broadbent, told Daniel, as he stepped deferentially to one side in order to admit Martha, who was carrying a paper bag from which a delicious-smelling steam was still rising.

'Two mutton pies for your dinner, from the bakery next door,' Martha announced as she handed the bag over with a loving smile. 'I know you're busy on delivery days and I didn't want you to have any excuse to nip down the road to that dreadful Black Swan. We're having pork for supper, so you won't be eating the same thing twice in one day.'

Daniel thanked her and invited her to rest on the chair in front of his desk. As she busied herself in examining her shopping list and ticking off, with the aid of a pen from Daniel's desk, the items she had already acquired, he reminded himself how lucky he was to have found such happiness and success, not only in his material life but also in his choice of a wife. She would shortly pass the milestone of her fortieth year, several months behind Daniel, but she was still strikingly handsome. Her hair was no longer a torrent of flowing black locks, but had been trimmed neatly into the nape of her neck to suit the climate and it contained streaks of the purest white here and there. But that only made her look more ladylike and her green eyes had not clouded over with age, but could still pierce a man with their clarity and haughty challenge.

Her figure had grown more matronly with childbirth, but somehow the ample bosom went so perfectly with the broadening hips that it was as if they had been coach-built to the last symmetrical inch. But as ever, it was her personality and zest for life that made her impossible to ignore and demanded the attention of everyone she addressed, male or female. One could not look upon Martha, or listen, entranced, to her ringing, melodic voice without remembering her for a long while thereafter. He was the luckiest man alive, he reminded himself and their children were blessed with the most naturally gifted mother in New South Wales.

'Why are you staring at me like that?' she asked him, tolerant amusement written across her face.

He smiled back. 'Just reminding myself of how beautiful you are.'

'Do you think I look my age?' she asked with a slight frown, 'or could I look to be in my early twenties if I applied enough cosmetic?'

'To me you'll always look like that girl I pulled off the deck of the *Lady Penrhyn*,' he replied gallantly. 'The young woman who ripped all my clothes off in the back room of the cottage next to George and Esther's.'

She blushed. 'I *was* rather eager that night, wasn't I?'

'You still are, some nights,' he reminded her. 'I just hope that three children will prove to be our full complement.'

'Which brings me back to the question you haven't answered yet,' she reminded him. 'Could I pass for a girl of twenty-something?'

'Probably, given your skill with make-up and your ability to be anyone you choose,' Daniel conceded, 'but why do you need to know?'

'Just curious,' she replied as she dropped her gaze to the bundles at her feet. 'Anyway, this won't get the supplies in. I still have to go back up the road to the gown shop. I took the carriage, by the way, and it's waiting for me outside. I take it that you came in on horseback, since I saw Ajax tied up outside — is that OK?'

'Of course, my dear. The latest gowns went up the road earlier today, so if you lose no more time, you'll get the best pick.'

'Thank you, sweetheart. Hopefully Elizabeth won't be in town until tomorrow or later, so I can make her frightfully jealous with the latest London fashion on my back when we go for supper tomorrow.'

'Tomorrow?' Daniel replied with a groan. 'This is the first time you've mentioned it and you know that I need at least a week's notice in order to prepare my immortal soul for another encounter with "Lady" Macarthur and all her vanities.'

'She didn't tell *me* until yesterday, when I went over to... Yes, well anyway, it's tomorrow. She's got all the latest gossip from London, it seems, and will simply explode if she's not allowed to recount it, blow by blow. So enjoy your mutton pies. I'd better scurry back up the road before it gets any hotter.'

A peck on the cheek and she was off, leaving Daniel wondering why she had paid a visit to Elizabeth Farm without even mentioning it to him and why she had stopped midway through a sentence, as if she was about to reveal more than she wished. It wasn't the first time that she'd seemed to be keeping something back from him lately and it made him uneasy.

He needed to stretch his legs, so he stood up and walked to the window, looking down from his upper storey office into the bustling street below. He noticed, with surprise, that the coach was still outside, with their coachman Devlin still seated with the reins hanging loosely in his hands, pipe-smoke wreathing upwards into the warm morning air. Then Daniel looked to the side and was puzzled to see Martha deep in conversation with two men. The older one looked familiar enough, but the younger one to whom Martha appeared to be giving the most animated attention was a stranger. He was tall, handsome and self-assured, and Daniel felt a pang of insecure jealously as he gazed down at his wife giving 'the treatment', as he called it, to a man half her age. Then he recalled her earlier question about her seeming desire to look as if she were in her early twenties and the uncomfortable feeling deepened.

'Here's the sales invoice for the chandler's store, sir. If you could sign it immediately, the carter's ready at the back door to take the consignment away.'

Daniel turned round to where Jim Broadbent stood, the invoice in his hand, and he beckoned him to join him at the window.

'Who are those two men down there with Mrs. Bradbury?' he asked.

Jim took off his spectacles and peered down. 'The older one's Robert Sidaway, sir. He owns the bakery next door. I'm surprised you had to ask, since he was in here only a few days ago with Mrs. Bradbury, while you were down on the quayside with Major Johnston. They seemed to be taking floor measurements and Mr. Sidaway was most inquisitive regarding how empty the lower floor gets between shipments. I hope I did the right thing by letting them in, sir, only with it being Mrs. Bradbury…'

'Yes, that's fine, Jim, don't worry yourself about it. No doubt she'll tell me in due course. But who's the younger man?'

'Never seen him before in my entire life, sir. Handsome cove, isn't he?'

'Depends on your tastes, I imagine,' Daniel replied curtly, then returned to his desk, signed the invoice, watched his floor manager disappear back down the stairs and sat wondering.

His mind wandered back to the days before he and Martha had finally got together and his fear of committing his heart to a woman who would remain beautiful while he aged. A woman who now seemed anxious to appear younger than she was and was plying her charm on a handsome young stranger in the street. A woman, what's more, who made visits to friends without telling her husband. Should he be paying her more attention, or perhaps making discreet enquiries instead of instinctively trusting her? After all, her life before he met her had been largely a succession of deceits and dishonesty and there was a well-known saying about leopards and spots.

21

The following evening Daniel was studying Martha's face closely as he tried to block out Elizabeth Macarthur's river of gossipy drivel following the receipt by her, from the *Parramatta*, of the latest letters from her society friends back in London. He was praying for the meal to end, the port bottle to appear and the ladies to withdraw, leaving George and John free to discuss business with him.

'Depend upon it,' Elizabeth was insisting, 'his days out here are numbered.'

'He almost seems to think so himself,' George confirmed, 'although he'd rather go on his own terms than be dismissed from office.'

Governor King seemed to be in a hopeless spiral, from which the Sydney English Exchange Institute was benefitting handsomely. The official word from London was to encourage all trade and commerce, while the unofficial order was to suppress what was seen as the growing commercial predominance of military officers who were neglecting their official duties in order to grow fat. The more that King followed the official line, the greater the number of letters of complaint winging their way back to London regarding the 'overweening arrogance' of the officers and men of the New South Wales Corps and their monopoly over rum supplies.

The truth was that rum was only the excuse, the symbol of much more that was wrong with the colonial economy. Men like Johnston and Macarthur had long since abandoned the rum trade after its initial success, together with craftily-acquired land grants, had facilitated the more secure trade in livestock and fleeces. Those who had not been granted the wide acres needed for such activities, and particularly those who had sought to make their own fortunes in the development of the new colony, were the ones now bleating back to Whitehall about being blocked by those ahead of them, who in the main were army officers. Since it was known that legitimate trading and commercial expansion were being encouraged in government circles back in London, it was necessary to focus the complaints on other areas of alleged mismanagement, and the obvious targets were the military officers who appeared to run things in open defiance of the governor and who were allegedly trading in human misery by their stranglehold on spirituous liquor in an age in which virtuous sobriety was the touchstone of a Christian community.

'Do you think he'll be allowed to go quietly?' Elizabeth asked eagerly.

George frowned before answering. 'That will depend upon majority opinion in London circles, about which you no doubt know more than I do,' he replied guardedly. 'But "better the Devil you know", as the saying goes and at least we seem to have managed to tie the current incumbent in knots. If we're not careful, they may replace him with someone who's not so easily managed.'

'When I was in London,' Macarthur chimed in, 'there was much talk of a Captain Bligh, who survived a mutiny on board his ship and some were voicing the opinion that he might be just the man to kick us all into shape. Of course they believe all that rubbish about the military running affairs out here, when as we well know it's the likes of George and myself. The leading lights in London don't seem to have fully grasped that the real source of our power runs on four feet.'

Governor King was finally relieved of his command in August 1806 and as John had predicted, his replacement was the stern disciplinarian William Bligh. Public confidence in his predecessor had sunk so low that the incoming Bligh was delighted to be greeted with addresses of welcome, one from George on behalf of the military men who guarded his colony and another from John Macarthur, on behalf of the 'free settlers' for whom he claimed to speak. However, it was not long before the suspicion began to form in Bligh's mind that a knife was pointed between his shoulder blades, when he received letters from other free settlers that left him in no doubt that Johnston and Macarthur were not to be trusted and that they would undermine his rule of the colony just as they had King's.

In the meantime, Daniel had increasing worries of his own. He had tried to banish to the back of his mind his initial unease regarding Martha's desire to look like a woman in her twenties and her animated conversation with the handsome young man outside the bakery and had almost succeeded until one day a few months later, when he was being driven home in the family coach. As they approached the front gates he was aware of someone galloping a fast horse out through the entrance and as he looked back in surprise he thought he recognised the same young man, head down and seemingly anxious to put some distance between himself and Haberfield House.

He climbed down from the coach and unusually Martha was not there to greet him with a kiss and a detailed description of what cook had prepared for supper. Instead there was only a morose-looking Matthew, bowling a hoop up and down the section of the drive immediately in front of the front entrance. Daniel put his arm around him and Matthew snuggled up to him as usual and attempted to demonstrate his burgeoning skills as a pickpocket by fumbling in Daniel's waistcoat pocket for loose change. Biting back the desire to advise him that practices such as that had led to his mother coming out to Australia in the first place, Daniel pushed his eager fingers away and asked of him casually, 'Who was that man I just saw leaving?'

'I don't know, but Mama got very angry when I went into the drawing room and found them sitting together on the settle. He was telling her that he must "make her his own" and she was agreeing with him. When they saw me in the doorway, Mama shouted at me to go outside, because she was busy.'

Daniel sat with a stony face throughout supper and Martha was apprehensive of asking the reason, for fear that something depressing to do with the business might be spoken in front of the children. Matthew was clearly already a little subdued from the earlier incident and Rebecca was old enough to be aware of a bad atmosphere. Fortunately Martha was able to busy herself trying to persuade Mark to eat his fish pie rather than spit it back all over her.

Finally, after the supper table had been cleared, Martha found Daniel in the drawing room, staring at the wall. She sat next to him and took his hand. 'There's obviously something bothering you, dearest. Is it to do with the business?'

'Who was that man who visited you today?' Daniel demanded bluntly.

She hesitated, then replied. 'His name is Michael Hargreave, why?'

'What precisely was he doing here, might I ask?'

Every second for which she delayed answering was like a whiplash to his brain. Finally she responded lamely with 'I'm not allowed to tell you.'

Daniel shot from the settle and glared back down at her. 'A man visits this house while I'm absent, tells you he wants to make you his own and you're "not allowed to tell me"? Not allowed by *who*, exactly?'

Her eyes dropped in confusion down to the carpet. 'I've been sworn to secrecy, but you'll find out soon enough. Let's leave it at that, shall we? Or am I to believe that our marriage vows mean so little to you that you suspect me of being unfaithful?'

'Wouldn't *you*, in my position?'

Martha gave a strangled cry and rushed from the room and then the house. When she returned two hours later, soaking wet from the unseasonal evening downpour, she refused to tell Daniel where she had been and was asleep by the time he came to bed.

The atmosphere in the house was frigid for days afterwards and Daniel was therefore not in the best of moods when a clerk from the governor's office arrived one day to advise him that, in accordance with the terms of the lease under which the Sydney English Exchange Institute occupied the former Commissary Store, the governor was exercising his power to occupy it for colonial purposes for a week commencing on 1st October. This gave Daniel only three weeks to make the necessary arrangements for the running of the business while the premises were closed, and on his way back down the High Street he stopped off at the Domain in search of George, hoping that he could shed some light on what was going on.

He was advised that George was at home, so he ordered the coachman to drive to Annandale. He stepped out of the coach and was admitted into the house by a wary-looking Sarah Biddle. As he walked down the hall, he could see directly into the rear garden through the full-length window at the foot of the staircase and there was the man Martha had identified as Michael Hargreave, heading down the lawn towards where George's service cutter was waiting to take him away.

George looked embarrassed as Daniel was shown into the sitting room, where he sat in his civilian clothes with Esther *and* Martha. Papers were noisily but surreptitiously slipped under the table between them and Daniel glared suspiciously at George.

'Do you have any idea why the governor's commandeered our business office for a week?'

'Yes,' Esther replied, just as George simultaneously replied 'No'. Martha turned bright red with embarrassment and Daniel glared back at Esther.

'Well?' he demanded, but it was George who offered the reply.

'We know that he requires it for government purposes, but he hasn't told us why.'

'And you just let him do it — without, I might add, even *informing* me?'

'I *was* going to tell you, obviously,' George replied, 'but Martha told us that you had a lot on your mind at the moment and I didn't want to add to your problems.'

'I wasn't aware that I *had* any problems,' Daniel spat back, 'so thank you for being more honest with me than my own wife. I'll see you back at home for supper,' he added with a curt nod towards Martha before turning on his heel and storming out.

When Martha returned home she chided Daniel for the rudeness of his departure from Annandale, and the atmosphere between them got even worse when Martha refused to tell him why Michael Hargreave had been meeting with her at Annandale and then declined Daniel's invitation to take two horses on a three-day sightseeing trip out west while the Institute was closed under the governor's order.

A week before the scheduled business break, Daniel asked their housekeeper to have the coach brought to the front door in order that he might travel into Sydney, only to be told that Martha had taken the coach two hours earlier, without telling him, or even enquiring as to whether or not he might need it that day.

He ordered his horse from the stable and rode it hard down the road into the town. As he approached the Institute, he first of all noted that the family coach was further down the road, then became aware of men carrying lengths of wood and canvas through the front door, while Jim Broadbent sat on an empty barrel to the side of the door, smoking his pipe. He stood up as he saw Daniel riding towards him with a stern expression on his face and walked over to where the horse was being tied to the railing.

'What's going on?' Daniel demanded. 'We've still got some deliveries to make from that last shipment.'

'Only a few cases,' Jim reminded him. 'They're up in your office, so that the ground floor can be cleared.

'Cleared for *what*, precisely?' Daniel demanded.

'No idea, sir. That man who's in there says it's got the governor's approval, so I just left them to it.'

Daniel brushed past him and stormed through the front door that gave access to the ground floor of the premises. Michael Hargreave was directing several men who were erecting some sort of platform at the end of the large room, which was otherwise empty. The door to Jim Broadbent's tiny office was lying open and from within it could be heard the sound of hammering.

'What the hell do you think you're playing at?' Daniel demanded.

Hargreave turned from supervising the labourers with a languid stare as he sized Daniel up and down. 'And who might *you* be?' he asked.

'Daniel Bradbury, partner in the Institute whose premises you seem to have commandeered. *And* the husband of the lady you've been seeing rather too much of in recent weeks. So unless you want to lose your teeth, you'd better begin explaining yourself!'

'Please forgive my husband,' came a soft and familiar voice as Martha stepped out from Jim's office, 'but he learned rough manners when he was a marine and they obviously haven't improved since. Daniel, meet Michael Hargreave.'

'I know only too well who *he* is!' Daniel bellowed. 'What I want to know now is what he's doing with *my* wife, in *my* business premises, behind *my* back!'

'It's easily explained…' Hargreave began, before Martha interrupted him.

'But it doesn't *need* to be, Michael. My husband can be very childish when he takes it upon himself and he clearly thinks that you and I are conducting an affair. Because he's so stubborn when he's in one of these moods, you could stand there all day trying to convince him otherwise, to no avail. Now, Daniel, if you'll excuse us, we're behind schedule already. I'll no doubt have to explain this all to you over supper, since you clearly won't give up until you get the answer you think you're entitled to.'

'It'll be supper for one, I'm afraid,' Daniel said as he turned on his heel. 'Give me time to get some belongings from the house and you can have the damned place all to yourself, for you *and* your fancy man here. Good afternoon to the pair of you!'

22

Daniel sat on the beach at Botany Bay, staring at the incoming tide and reflecting on his finest achievement — the bringing in of Bennelong. Nobody had thought him a coward that day, the day he'd won Martha her ticket of leave, freeing her from convict labour into convict service.

He heard the sound of a footstep on the shingle behind him. He spun round and there stood George.

'I suppose Martha sent you? Conscience got the better of her, did it?'

'I have to get you to accept my word that Martha hasn't been unfaithful to you with Michael Hargreave. We've *all* been guilty of deceiving you and what was meant as a pleasant surprise has all gone horribly wrong. Just trust me far enough to come to the Macarthurs' place; Martha can join you there and she can tell you as much as she chooses to. Please, Daniel, trust me this one more time.'

Daniel let George lead him to the Macarthurs. As they sat on the back veranda with a jug of wine and a basket of Elizabeth's home-made biscuits, Daniel appeared to be finally convinced that Martha and Michael Hargreave were not conducting an affair, but argued that he was entitled to some explanation of their suspicious behaviour.

'We're putting on a play,' Martha explained. 'It was originally Elizabeth's idea. You know how obsessed she is with anything to do with the theatre and what an insufferable social climber she is —' this said in a lowered voice, following a backward glance to confirm the absence of any audience — 'Anyway, she came up with the idea of putting on a play to welcome the new governor and got him to agree to the use of the Institute as a theatre. She also found out — don't ask me how — that Robert Sidaway, before he became the baker next door to you and before he became a convict, was an actor. Anyway, to cut a long story short, Michael Hargreave is his nephew and, as luck would have it, the current rave of Drury Lane, everyone's favourite leading man. He's out here visiting his uncle and was prevailed upon to take the leading role. It was meant as a surprise for you, but it just got worse and worse when we told lie after lie. Will you come and watch the play?'

Daniel kissed her. 'I'm just so glad that you weren't unfaithful to me that right now I'd agree to anything.'

She gripped his hand. 'I don't know *how* you could possibly have thought that I'd been conducting an affair with that conceited popinjay, although I suppose it *did* look suspicious. But how could you have believed that George and Esther were covering up for me? We should have let you in on it weeks ago, and once you came across us setting up the theatre that was obviously the time to own up. But you were your own worst enemy when you got all angry with Michael — you reminded me of my stepfather with your domineering manner and it brought it all back to me. I'm afraid that brought out the worst in me and you know how I can get when I think I'm being challenged or demeaned in some way — like when I thought you'd bought my freedom.'

'No need to apologise — it was my fault for getting jealous and possessive. I think I'm the luckiest man alive and I can't wait to see this play you're producing.'

'I'm not actually the producer — Elizabeth claimed that role and Robert's been directing.'

'So what's your part in it all?'

'You'll see. I have to leave for Sydney in the morning to set things up. Elizabeth will be coming back with me, and you can spend a few days here, then travel in with John; you'll be able to talk business and the Institute's closed anyway, while we put up all the scenery. We'll need to commandeer every chair in the colony, because we reckon we can seat almost two hundred. You have a reserved seat on the front row.'

'And will you be there?'

'Of course, but I'll be busy. You wouldn't believe how much work goes into staging a production.'

The next morning Martha set off back to Haberfield with a promise to have Devlin return with Daniel's clothing and shaving equipment, in return for Daniel's promise to wear his best suit for the production, and Daniel and Macarthur occupied most of the day going over business plans. Daniel was anxious to ensure that they still had a secure future and asked Macarthur what he knew about the new governor and his likely attitude towards the Institute.

Macarthur frowned. 'I think this new man Bligh may be made of sterner stuff than King. The last three governors were removed from office because of their inability to face up to the military component of the colony, but Bligh's already proved that he can put down uppity sailors and I think that London hopes he'll do the same with former soldiers running businesses out here. Back in London they seem convinced that it's all about rum and it suits Bligh to let them think that. But something tells me that he can see the fuller picture and we have to be doubly careful not to give him any excuse to undermine our farming interests. He's under pressure from smaller concerns that are jealous of our pre-eminence and they're the ones writing all the poisonous letters back home.

Anyway, just make sure that we don't transgress any stupid laws — that's just the excuse he'd need to cut us down to the size he thinks we should be.'

'Have you settled the matter of your land grant over in Camden?'

'No, that's still being debated. Bligh's latest argument is that it's the best pasture in the colony and that he needs it for government cattle — which is a better argument than King ever came up with. But as long as my fleeces and carcases are bringing money into the colony, I hope that the Colonial Office will see the sense of letting me keep it, as well as saving face over the original grant that Camden gave me.'

Three days later, John and Daniel took the Macarthur coach back down the well-worn track to Sydney along the Parramatta Road. Daniel paused briefly at Haberfield in order to leave his belongings, hug the children and thank Lucy for the excellent job she was doing with them, then hopped back into the coach. As they trotted along the High Street, Daniel was amazed at the transformation of the outside of the Institute, the former Commissary Store that he remembered so well from the earliest days in which he was grappling with his emotions regarding the young Martha Mallett. He looked up at the massive canvas poster hanging above the entrance, announcing:

INSTITUTE PRODUCTIONS
FOR ONE NIGHT ONLY
PRESENTS
"Love for Love", by William Congreve
Tickets 2/- and 1/-, available at door,
or in advance from Harbour Bakery
Full London cast

Daniel was wondering how they could possibly justify the claim to a 'full London cast', unless they were all former convict actors who had fallen upon hard times, like the baker next door. But his thoughts were distracted as he entered the hall and saw the three-foot-high stage that had been constructed at the far end, with a pair of heavy drape curtains and areas on either side that had been screened off and were presumably what they called the 'wings', through which the actors and actresses made their entry and exit. He'd attended the theatre a few times during his Bristol days along with a friend who had pretensions to be a playwright and he had a rudimentary knowledge of how it all worked.

Elizabeth was ushering people to their seats up at the front and she waved furiously in order to gain their attention, beckoning for Daniel and Macarthur to move down to the front row. 'The first seat here on the right is for the governor,' she instructed them in her best bossy tone, 'then you, John, and then Daniel.'

'Where will George and Esther be sitting?' Daniel asked.

'You'll see soon enough,' Elizabeth replied. 'And before you ask, Martha will be out once we get into the Second Act.'

'Should I save her a seat?' Daniel asked.

'She has her own,' was the enigmatic reply, as Elizabeth recognised someone else of colonial importance and waved to them before bustling off in their direction.

There was a programme on every seat and Daniel took his, sat down and opened it. The play was in five acts, apparently, and the opening page was devoted to a cast list that was pompously headed '*Dramatis Personae*'. Daniel read it with deep interest, chuckling from time to time at the depth of the deception to which he'd been subjected.

SIR SAMPSON LEGEND, *father to Valentine and Ben* — Mr. Robert Sidaway

VALENTINE, *his son* — Mr. Michael Hargreave

SCANDAL, *his friend* — Mr. Joseph Tremayne

TATTLE, *a half-witted beau* — Mr. Percy Froggett

BEN, *Sir Sampson's younger son* — Mr. William Bright

FORESIGHT, *an illiterate old fellow, uncle to Angelica* — Mr. George Johnston

JEREMY, *servant to Valentine* — Mr. Amos Black

TRAPLAND, *a scrivener* — Mr. Julian Freeman

BUCKRAM, *a lawyer* — Mr. Thomas Dance

ANGELICA, *niece to Foresight* — Miss Marianne Merchant

MRS. FORESIGHT, *second wife to Foresight* — Miss Caroline Blunt

MRS. FRAIL, *sister to Mrs. Foresight* — Miss Esther Julian

MISS PRUE, *daughter to Foresight by a former wife* — Miss Margaret Prentice

NURSE — Mrs. Elizabeth Macarthur

JENNY — Miss Anne Blenkhorn

The scenes: two houses in London

There was a rustle of activity as the governor was bowed into his front row seat by a beaming Elizabeth, who then mounted the short staircase at the side of the stage, walked to the centre of it and raised her hands for silence.

'Your Excellency, ladies and gentlemen, it gives me profound pleasure to welcome you here this evening, to the first of what we hope will prove to be many fine productions here at the Institute Theatre. The play you are about to see has been performed to excellent reviews in London's Drury Lane and was written by one of England's foremost Restoration playwrights, Mr. William Congreve.

'We are doubly fortunate to have here in the colony some fine dramatic talent and several seasoned actors who come to us from recent successes in Drury Lane itself. First of all, that doyen of the London scene, Mr. Michael Hargreave, who will be playing the leading role of our hero, aptly named "Valentine". Playing the role of his father is Mr. Robert Sidaway, who some of you will recognise as your local baker, but who had a distinguished career on the stage before circumstances brought him out here among us.

'But most exciting of all is the presence on stage of our leading lady this evening, Miss Marianne Merchant, who was for several years a leading Drury Lane actress. She has been resident in the colony now for several years and only disclosed her previous experience to me — I have to shamefully admit, in confidence — during one of my regular social gatherings. She is this evening playing the leading lady role of Angelica and I would ask you to be most appreciative of her generosity in allowing us to enjoy such a cultural experience in this new land of ours. Ladies and Gentlemen, "Love for Love".'

Elizabeth stepped to the side with a gracious wave towards the curtains. The play progressed through what seemed, to Daniel at least, to be very short scenes, all with the same scenery and setting. Since there was no indication of when each act of the play began and ended, Daniel had no way of knowing when Martha would be joining him as promised, in the seat that he had carefully kept vacant for her by his side. The opening and closing of each scene was indicated by the drawing and reopening of the curtains and the only break occurred after just under an hour or so, when noises behind the drawn curtains suggested that scenery was being changed.

Sure enough, when the curtain rose yet again, there was George, heavily made up to look like a much older man, who was loudly demanding, of a servant, the whereabouts of various relatives, including his niece. Then a beautiful young woman entered, with a request to borrow his coach for 'pleasure' and Daniel's jaw dropped when he heard the melodic, almost hypnotic, voice of the woman who for the past twenty years had made his life worth living.

She was wearing a massive wig with long fair curls trailing down to the bodice of her gown and she was heavily made up to look like the 'flighty' young girl she was portraying, but there was no mistaking the penetrating green eyes. In total astonishment, he checked the programme that he had earlier stuffed into his pocket and chuckled. Not only was Martha acting the role of an inconsequential young heiress, but she was also doing so under the assumed name of 'Marianne Merchant'. Whether or not she had fooled Elizabeth that this had been her professional name during the Drury Lane career that she'd never had was neither here nor there — the audience believed it and they were lapping up her performance.

Now it all made sense. The frequent absences from home, the furtive meetings with Michael Hargreave, when they were no doubt rehearing scenes from the play unfolding before him, the refusal to disclose what was really going on in the Institute while the governor had it closed — it all added up and he was the biggest, brashest, most clod-hopping fool of a man who ever lived, with a wife who was a talented, gifted, beautiful angel of a woman he would never doubt again.

As the curtains were drawn at the end of the closing scene, there was tumultuous applause from the appreciative audience and the curtains were pulled back once more to reveal the entire cast on stage. After several bows, two young girls wobbled uncertainly up the side steps to present bouquets of flowers to both Martha and Elizabeth, who was still in costume after her performance as the nurse. Elizabeth walked proudly off the stage and to further applause presented her bouquet to the governor, who rose to kiss her on the cheek. Daniel looked back at where Martha was beaming down at him with an exultant grin; suddenly she pouted him a kiss and threw her bouquet down to him. He caught it deftly and blew a kiss back at her; even from that distance he could see the tears carving channels into her heavy make-up.

An hour or so later, after the audience had dispersed, the actors came out from behind the curtain, some of them still wiping off their make-up. Elizabeth was the first to reach the front row, where she was embraced by John. She looked over John's shoulder at Daniel and asked, 'Was it worth all the deception?'

'Most definitely,' he replied, 'but "full London cast"?'

'They all came from London, originally,' Elizabeth replied with a wry grin.

'Some of them as convicts, no doubt,' Daniel replied.

'And they call *me* a snob!' Elizabeth retorted, as Daniel was almost barrelled to the floor by Martha in a big bear hug.

'Did you prefer me with fair hair?' she asked breathlessly.

'Definitely not,' he replied, 'but after that triumph, I'll no doubt have to get used to seeing my wife transformed.'

23

Despite their frequent and enthusiastic endeavours, Daniel and Martha had no more children. But by the start of 1808 it was as if they had combined the Bradbury household with that of the Johnstons, who occupied the adjoining property to theirs and whose mansion was less than a mile up the road and the briefest of coach trips either way.

Martha had become increasingly critical of the education that her children were receiving from a succession of indifferent home tutors, whereas Esther was forever singing the praises of the one who attended at Annandale every day to instil some education into her lively brood. His name was Emrys Jones and he had been a teacher in a very select private boys' school in the Buckinghamshire village of Amersham until he fell into temptation regarding the school funds, which he needed for additional nursing services for his invalid widowed mother. The sum had been a large one, but the judge had taken into account the man's learning and decided that the new colony of New South Wales might benefit from his services once his seven-year term expired, as it had a year before he was recommended to George by the Reverend Marsden.

He was a gifted teacher of children and even the haughty and somewhat headstrong Roseanna had been persuaded to improve her English to the point at which she was regularly reading novels as she curled beneath the spreading gum trees dotted around the front lawn. George Junior, now approaching nineteen, had no interest in anything without a saddle, while his younger brother Robert had already declared his future to be in the Navy, for which Latin and Greek would be something of a superfluity.

The real scholar among the Johnston brood appeared to be David, approaching nine years old and the constant companion of his somewhat less studious neighbour Rebecca Bradbury, upon whom he nevertheless appeared to exercise some intellectual influence. It was their obvious mutuality and the similarities in their ages and intellectual development, that first led to Martha's suggestion that Rebecca should transfer her studies up the road, where the tutoring was of a higher quality. This was rapidly agreed to, in the hope that the presence of Rebecca would be a good socialising influence on Julia and Blanche as she undertook regular education and left the nursery to her younger sister Maria, with the middle sister Isabella somewhere between the two.

Once Rebecca had made the switch, it made economic good sense for her to be joined by her sixteen-year-old brother Matthew, for his final year of education before he pursued what seemed to be his determination to join the Army. At the combined schoolroom in Annandale, Matthew and Rebecca would in due course be joined by their brother Mark, who, at two years of age, still required a nurse rather than a tutor.

The ongoing need for a nurse in both houses had also added to what seemed like a marriage between two families. With only Maria Johnston requiring a full-time nurse, the onerous duties that had led to Sarah Biddle being assisted by Lucy Bracegirdle no longer required the work of two and Mark Bradbury was so enamoured of Lucy that arrangements were well under way for her to transfer to Haberfield House as nurse/deputy housekeeper when the Johnston coachman, Edward Tolhurst, threw a squib into proceedings by proposing marriage to her.

George reacted with predictable calm and generosity by not only hosting their wedding reception on the front lawns of Annandale, but also agreeing to Tolhurst's transfer to Haberfield, with the former Bradbury coachman, Devlin, replacing him at Annandale. This complex domestic merger was rounded off by the conversion of the former rudimentary schoolroom at the back of Haberfield House into a head office for the Institute, leaving John Macarthur's older son Edward to supervise the physical side of things in the Sydney office, in his mother's hope that the ambitions he had developed during his education back in England to become an Army officer would evaporate in the heat of commerce.

It was an appropriate time for those engaged in the business of the Institute to have all hands on deck, given the seeming determination of the new governor, Bligh, to trim its sails. His first action following the successful staging of Elizabeth's first venture into drama production had been to summon George into his office at the Domain in order to lay down the ground rules.

George had not been invited to take a seat, so he remained at attention as Bligh left him in no doubt of the future agenda.

'Please congratulate your good lady on a first class production the other evening. And you weren't too shabby yourself, although I hope that the drivelling buffoon you were depicting was not intended as a lampoon of me.'

'Absolutely not, sir,' George assured him with his straightest face, while looking dead ahead at the wall behind the governor.

'Very well, now down to business. Let there be no doubt in anyone's mind that *I* run this colony, not you and your men. I'm aware that my predecessor gave you some additional land out in Cabramatta in gratitude for the job that you did out at Rose Hill, suppressing those rebellious scum who clearly had no gratitude for the mercy they had already been shown, but I wish that in no way to be employed as a precedent, do you understand? You are paid to protect me and my colony, along with your men and now that Paterson has been sent to enforce the King's peace in Van Diemen's Land, you are effectively the commanding officer of the entire Corps. It is your sworn duty to ensure that the colony remains peaceful and law-abiding and that your men are reminded of the loyalty they owe to me. To *me*, do you understand? Not you — *me*. You cannot expect further grants of land upon which to grow rich through cattle production merely for performing the duty for which you are paid a Major's salary. Understood?'

'Yes, sir. Completely, sir.'

'Very well — dismiss.'

Although George was the first to experience the rough edge of Bligh's tongue, others would not have to wait long. The new governor was one of those men with the inherent ability to cause trouble in an empty room, and he soon locked horns with John Macarthur when he gave away beasts from the colony's herds and supplies from its stores, to farmers in dire need after severe flooding on the Hawkesbury, in return from an undertaking that they would in future do no business with either Macarthur or the Institute of which he was a partner. When Macarthur protested, he was very rudely reminded that the governor was acting in the best interests of the colony as a whole, and not those who had grown fat by exploiting it.

Another vitriolic letter from Elizabeth to a very highly placed friend in London was the first warning to the Colonial Office that they might not have chosen wisely in placing the colony under the iron fist of an arrogant, hard-nosed martinet who might be very good at hanging and flogging naval ratings, but knew little about diplomacy. There was a further shaking of aristocratic heads in high places when Bligh himself wrote back to London that he had placed a total embargo on the use of rum as a medium of exchange and was expecting a strong resistance that might even develop into a full-scale rebellion; however, he assured them, he would meet such a response with all the armed force at his disposal.

The Institute and its partners were not the only ones to doubt the wisdom of Bligh's appointment. His approach to justice was a very personalised one, beginning with condoning the trial of a group of Irish convicts on capital 'revolt' charges by a court that consisted of their accusers. Somehow or other, despite this, the men were acquitted anyway and Bligh refused to have them released from custody. He also dismissed from magisterial office the highly capable Surgeon-General of the colony, Thomas Jamison, for no other obvious reason than the fact that he was a business associate of Macarthur's. He followed this up by dismissing, again without any reason with a vestige of credibility, the colony's Assistant Surgeon D'Arcy Wentworth and gave free vent to his ill temper by fining and imprisoning three local merchants who had penned a letter to London that he regarded as offensive to his dignity.

As if to show that his venom was not class based, he also antagonised large numbers of the lower middle class who had begun to find their feet in their new land by ordering them to dismantle and remove houses they had built on land they rented from the colony. Little wonder that as early as October of the previous year, George Johnston, as the commanding officer of the New South Wales Corps, had written to his ultimate commanding officer, the Commander-in-Chief of the British Army, warning him that it was to be doubted if he could, for much longer, stand by and watch his men being verbally abused by the man they were sworn to defend, or ignore the interference, by a naval officer, with the work of a land army.

The powder keg awaited only a match and this was supplied at the very start of 1808, when Bligh was presented with an opportunity to put John Macarthur in his place. It was a minor technicality, but it led to an armed uprising against Bligh.

The first indication of what was to come had landed on Daniel's desk the previous month. It was official notification, from the governor's office, that the Institute was to forfeit the seven-hundred-pound bond that had, in accordance with colonial regulations, been lodged with the Transit Board in security of the compliance of the master and crew of the *Parramatta* with all colonial laws. A convict had succeeded in stowing away below decks while the vessel had been moored in Sydney Harbour and when Macarthur advised the governor, on behalf of the Institute, that he was disputing the legality of the forfeiture, Bligh ordered Judge-Advocate Richard Atkins to summon Macarthur to his court to argue the point. When Macarthur arrogantly failed to appear on the due day, Bligh ordered his arrest. He was granted bail, on condition that he appear to answer a charge of contempt of court on 25th January.

Macarthur objected to the court that was to try him being headed by Judge-Advocate Atkins, on the ground that Atkins owed him a business debt. Atkins refused to step down on that ground and in response the officers of the Corps who had been empanelled as a jury, in accordance with contemporary practice, walked out in sympathy with Macarthur's objection. Bligh ordered Macarthur's re-arrest and when the officers of the Corps responded by demanding a new Judge-Advocate and the release of Macarthur from custody, the governor demanded that George attend at his Mansion and give him a good reason why his Corps officers should not themselves be charged with mutiny.

A hasty council of war was summoned around the large dining table at Annandale. It consisted not only of George and Daniel and their wives, but also Elizabeth Macarthur, who was invited to stay at Haberfield House while John was languishing in the town's gaol. Elizabeth Farm was being managed, for the time being, by Edward Macarthur, freed from his Institute duties, and it was a highly indignant Elizabeth who opened the proceedings with the complaint that her husband's extensive business interests now required the supervision of a son barely into his twenties whose real ambitions were military.

'Please God that all this nonsense puts any idea of army service out of his head. No disrespect to you, George, but it's come to a sorry pass when a man is faced with the terrible decision you have to make, simply because he's under the notional command of a tyrant.'

George looked like a man facing the gallows upon which he was about to be hanged, as he looked across the table at Daniel. 'What do you think I should do, Daniel? You're the lawyer.'

'No I'm not,' Daniel replied. 'At least, I have no experience of the sort of constitutional dilemma you're faced with, nor do I have any knowledge of criminal law. But it seems to me, if it's my opinion you're seeking, that the only basis for the allegation of mutiny against the men is that they refuse to obey the dictates of a man who's clearly lost all sense of proportion. Was it "mutiny" when the people of France rose up against their king?'

'You're not talking about armed rebellion, surely, George?' Esther gasped, a hand to her mouth in sheer horror. 'You could be hanged for that.'

George put his arm around her consolingly, but looked bleakly back across the table. 'Daniel has a point, I'm afraid. "Mutiny" has suddenly become anything that the governor disagrees with. We can't run a society on that basis — that would be like plunging us back under the Roman Emperors, or that dreadful Henry VIII. Provided that we strictly uphold the law of this colony, then we'll keep our noses clean and as I understand it, "mutiny" is any refusal to obey the orders of the King himself.'

'Bligh will argue that he *is* the King, in the sense that he carries his commission to govern the colony,' Daniel countered.

'But only in accordance with the laws of England,' George reminded him. 'The Magna Carta — if I recall my history correctly — gave every man the right to be judged and punished only by a jury of his peers and under a justice system that is unbiased. John was quite right to object to Atkins running the court when he owes him money and my men were well within *their* rights to refuse to serve under him. Tell me I'm wrong.'

'You're *not* wrong, George,' Elizabeth assured him, 'and may I remind you all that it's *my* husband who's sitting there chained to the wall?'

The next morning the entire Johnston family lined up at the front door to bid farewell to George and their tears and hugs conveyed the strong belief that he would not be coming back to them that evening. He was on his favourite mount, Pegasus, having left the carriage at home in case his family might need it in his absence and as he rode gloomily down the Parramatta Road towards the township that was clearly visible down the slope, he was aware of a faster mount catching up with his. He turned in the saddle and grinned as he saw Daniel only a few yards behind him. 'Going shopping?' he asked sardonically.

'Shopping for justice, let's say,' Daniel replied.

'This isn't your battle, Daniel, and you're not even a soldier any more.'

'Thanks to you and John. John's now in jail and you're about to do something as risky as I did at Botany Bay. The least I can do is to attempt to whip up the mob at the appropriate moment.'

'You'll do no such thing,' George argued back. 'Hopefully public opinion's with us anyway, in which case there'll be no need for a mob orator to lead the storming of the Bastille. If they're *not* with me, then they deserve the governor they've got.'

'And what about *you*, if they're not with you? As far as I can read your mind, I think you're about to lead a rebellion — I only hope that it's a popular one. We can worry about London later.'

George pulled in the reins and halted his horse and Daniel did likewise. 'Daniel, I appreciate the offer and I'd like to think that you'd follow me through the gates of Hell, but you have a wife and children back there, who need you. No point in us *both* ending up in jail, or on the end of a noose.'

Daniel looked across at him. 'I remember a man who walked up behind me on the beach at Botany, pulled me to my feet and took a pistol from me before I deprived myself of the rest of a very happy life. That life's yours now, George, if that's what it comes to.'

A tear began to form in George's eye as he fought for words of reply. When they didn't come, he gently urged his horse onwards. When he realised that Daniel was still alongside him he said, without looking round, 'You always *were* the stupidest, most unpredictable idiot that I was ever in command of, but you're also the best friend a man could wish for. You need your head examined, but let's keep going and see what transpires.'

As they rode down the High Street side by side, Daniel was surprised to see George reining in his horse at the front entrance to the Town Gaol and hitching it to a post, in clear view of a substantial crowd that had already gathered for what promised to be some free entertainment.

'Aren't you summoned to see the governor?' he asked.

'The governor will be seeing me soon enough,' George grimaced. 'First of all, I've decided to join John for breakfast.' As he headed with a determined stride up the front steps and demanded that the turnkeys on the door allow him to pass, several bystanders were curious.

'Is John Macarthur being released?' one of them asked.

Daniel remained in the saddle and looked down at the man. 'If there's any justice he will be,' he replied, 'or else we're all at risk. If the governor can get away with using the army to imprison an innocent man, just because he's envious of his money and success, then *none* of us is safe.'

After a few minutes George appeared through the front door of the gaol and trotted down the steps carrying several sheets of paper and a quill. From his dress jacket pocket he produced a small, sealed, container of ink and handed them all up to Daniel.

'You seem to have attracted quite a crowd already,' he observed to Daniel. 'I've ordered John's release from custody and he'll be out in a minute. He occupied his time drafting a petition, in his capacity as a leading man in the community, calling upon me to arrest the governor on a charge of treason against the King and his people. I'm off to collect some more men at the barracks — you might wish to occupy your time collecting some more signatures.'

With that he galloped off down the road, leaving Daniel to dismount and spread the petition out on top of one of the gateposts at the gaol entrance. He turned to face the rapidly growing crowd.

'Here we are then, gentlemen. Major Johnston, as most of you will know, is the commanding officer of our army and he's decided to take the brave stance of releasing John Macarthur from a totally unjustified spell in jail. If you don't want to be the next person that the governor picks on, you might wish to add your names to this petition for the man's removal from office. The soldiers are all on our side, which means that the governor can't do anything to hurt you if you sign and authorise the present governor's imprisonment pending the appointment of a new governor. Who wants to put their name down?'

He had over fifty signatures in no time and a queue had begun to form in front of the petition by the time that George reappeared with forty uniformed marines, some of them carrying the instruments they played in the recently formed Corps band. They added their names to the petition, then a grim-faced George ordered them into a square formation, with the band members at the front.

'Very well, men,' he shouted, to muted cheers from the civilians all around the gaol entrance, 'let's go and do our duty in execution of this valid petition.'

The column marched steadily up the dusty roadway towards Governor's Mansion. They came to a halt at the foot of the stairs leading to the front door, where a lady in her thirties, dressed in suitable clothing for a morning walk and struggling to open a parasol, regarded them stonily from the top step.

'My father hasn't completed his breakfast yet,' she told George, who was standing at the head of his contingent. 'You're blocking my way down the stairs.'

'And you, madam,' George told her in a commanding voice, 'are blocking *our* way *up* the stairs. We're here to arrest the governor.'

George marched his men up the stairs and through the front door. Once inside, they clomped down the polished floorboards and into the governor's office, which was empty. A search of the ground floor having yielded nothing, George sent Captain Laycock upstairs with three men in order to search the private rooms.

Laycock came down a few minutes later with a broad grin, holding a terrified-looking governor by the sleeve of his frock coat. He appeared to have had time to don his full dress uniform.

'I found him trying to hide under a bed, sir,' he told George.

'Nonsense!' Bligh proclaimed. 'I was merely hiding some papers of critical concern to the colony, since I was led by the servants to believe that an insurrection was in progress.'

'Not an insurrection, sir,' George told him, 'simply a changing of the guard at colonial level. You are my prisoner, on a charge of treason against His Majesty and his subjects, and will be held under house arrest until instructions can be obtained from London as to how you are to be further dealt with.'

'I'll make sure you hang for this!' Bligh bellowed.

'All in due course,' George replied calmly. 'For the moment, I require your undertaking that you will make no attempt to escape, otherwise you will be taken from here down to the town gaol, from which I recently released Mr. Macarthur.'

'More treason!' Bligh yelled, his face now as red as a turkey-cock.

'I can only be hanged once,' George observed. 'Now, if you would be so good as to hand over the keys to your despatch boxes and cabinets — and please bear in mind that, as the governor's *aide-de-camp* for so many years, I will be well aware if you attempt to withhold any.'

Bligh was led away, still spluttering and protesting, and George asked Thomas Laycock to find Daniel and bring him inside.

Daniel was led into the governor's office, where he smiled at the sight of George behind the large mahogany desk. 'It suits you,' he grinned.

George smiled back. 'Looks like I just became the King of New South Wales. If you wish to play the role of my court jester, I have a few tasks for you. The first is to ride back to Haberfield and bring Elizabeth back here to be reunited with John, for whom I also have a few tasks before they both go back to their property. Then please get Devlin to bring Esther up here to join me, since she just became the first — and probably the only — convict "first lady" in the history of the colony. Elizabeth will be beside herself with envy, but she can be the wife of my soon-to-be-appointed Colonial Secretary, reporting to his old friend the acting governor.'

Daniel looked concerned. 'How long do you think you can get away with all this?'

'For as long as it takes for London to respond to my first despatch, which will advise them of what's taken place today and of the existence of a senior vacancy in colonial administration. Don't let the *Parramatta* raise anchor without it.'

24

In the event, George settled for the title of 'Lieutenant-Governor', thereby publicly acknowledging that his was only a caretaker regime and that he was merely running things until London saw fit to replace Bligh. Once released, John Macarthur was endowed — to Elizabeth's considerable delight — with the newly created role of 'Colonial Secretary', which post he maximised for his own financial benefit and that of the Institute. He commissioned a second vessel, the *George*, which began a series of highly profitable circuits of the South Pacific that incorporated Canton, Calcutta, Bombay and Edo. The *Parramatta* continued the old cycle of trips to London via the Cape, and its master and crew barely had time to be reunited with their families after each landing in Sydney before being hustled off back to London.

The reason for the short turnarounds was not merely the need to maximise trade profits before those in London realised what was happening, but the desire to ensure a regular flow of despatches, the only forms of communication available. A despatch on an incoming journey carried the ironic promotion of George to the rank of lieutenant-colonel, before London had been advised that he had awarded himself a higher colonial rank. But, as Daniel had predicted, it could not last forever and on 28th July a government vessel landed another lieutenant-colonel, Joseph Foveaux, who carried a commission to act as governor.

George obediently, but proudly, handed over the reins of office, while John Macarthur returned to Elizabeth Farm ahead of supervising a new mansion out at Camden. Throughout this entire period, Daniel, with only limited assistance from Edward Macarthur, was run off his feet keeping goods coming and going from the Institute, organising 'runs' of cattle and sheep from Annandale and Elizabeth Farm and doubling the size of the ice-house at the foot of his rear garden.

The writing began to appear on the wall the following year, 1809, when Foveaux was replaced as acting governor by George and Daniel's old enemy, Lieutenant-Colonel Paterson. It was Paterson who kept prevailing upon London not to let the recent insurrection go unpunished or unrecognised, referring in despatch after despatch to what he termed 'The Rum Rebellion', even though the lowest minion in the Whitehall bureaucracy was well aware that the issues had been much broader than that. However, given that the alternative to alleging that the army had taken over in order to preserve their monopoly of liquor supplies was to openly admit that the fourth governor appointed by London in twenty years had proved to be an abject failure, the pretence was maintained and George was summoned back to London to be court-martialled.

There was another council of war at Annandale when the order came through. George Junior was both prepared and secretly delighted to be deputised to run the family cattle business and Daniel assured George that he would keep an avuncular eye on things, as well as ensuring the regular despatch of cattle and sheep to England and supplying to local shopkeepers on the usual wholesale terms. The real topic of debate, however, was whether or not John Macarthur should travel to London with George.

'If it's just George's word against those pen-pushing cretins in Whitehall,' John argued, 'he'll get buried. Please don't lose sight of the fact that one possible outcome of a finding of guilt in a court-martial on a charge of treason, or even mutiny, is a hanging.'

'That's all very noble of you, John,' Elizabeth responded coldly, 'but what about your business interests in the meantime?'

'Isn't that why we have two sons?' John replied.

Elizabeth treated them all to one of her snorts. 'Edward's only ambition is to join the Army, despite the fact that you were forced to resign — and let's not try to pretend that you weren't. As for James, he still has his education to complete and it might be better if you were to take him back to England, if you're so determined to ruin us financially by leaving the business at such a critical time. The only hope would seem to be to ask our nephew Hannibal to come back over here — he was clearly interested in the commercial side of things before John foolishly let him go back to England to pursue that rather unsuitable King girl after her father was removed as governor.'

'Hannibal doesn't have enough commercial experience,' John objected. 'It's not just a simple matter of a few flocks of sheep running over a few acres of pasturage any more — most of our money these days comes from the trading of sandalwood, rum, spices and shop goods on the round trips made by the *George*.'

'That's my department, surely,' Daniel pointed out. 'I clearly can't help you with the sheep, but if George Junior can handle the cattle side of it and Elizabeth can get a manager for the fleece trade, I'm pretty sure I can handle the extra charterparties and contracts.'

John reached out, took Elizabeth's hand in his and fixed her with a serious look. 'It may be our only way forward, dearest.'

Elizabeth looked uncertainly across at Daniel. 'Are you sure you could handle the pressure? After all, with John and George both missing and this new governor they're threatening us with, who sounds like the Devil in a red coat, you're going to be under the most *enormous* strain.'

Daniel smiled back at her. 'I owe everything I have today to George and John and their generosity in taking me into their business when I was at my most desperate and most needful. The least I can do is work a little harder to justify the faith they showed in me After all, if you insist that I'm not up to it, you're doubting the commercial wisdom of the most successful entrepreneur in the colony.'

John laughed lightly. 'You may not have had the smooth tongue of a lawyer when we first took you on, but by God you've made up for it since, man.' He looked back at Elizabeth, who was clearly wavering. 'Do we have a choice, if I'm to support, in his greatest hour of need, the man who stood discreetly to the side while I built up the enterprise that got me out of the Army — something you were always so insistent on?'

Elizabeth looked across the table. 'George? We're talking about you as if you weren't here — what do *you* think?'

George smiled. '"Misery doth acquaint a man with strange bedfellows" — isn't that how it goes?'

It was Elizabeth's turn to smile. '"Et tu, Brute?"' she replied and it was all settled bar the fine details.

The next five years tested them all in different ways. The most obvious burden was borne, patiently but with increasing emotional pain, by Esther, who cried almost non-stop for a week after George and John stepped on board the *Admiral Gambier* in late March 1809, heading for London. Her daughter Roseanna alerted Martha to the true extent of Esther's mental plight, and Martha insisted on moving into Annandale House as Esther's constant companion. She took four-year-old Mark with her, along with his nurse Lucy Tolhurst, who also agreed to act as chaperone and general ladies' maid to the growing Johnston girls; without anything further being said, the two family coachmen reverted to their former roles, in order that Lucy might remain with her husband.

This left eighteen-year-old Matthew potentially alone in the house with Mary, the cook/housekeeper to the Bradburys, until George's second son, Robert, decided it would be great fun to join his lifelong friend, who was approximately his age anyway, in somewhat juvenile 'scrapes' around the neighbourhood. This freed up another bedroom at Annandale, into which Esther installed David, while Rebecca took yet another bed in the female children's bedroom in the same house, which began to take on the appearance of a dormitory in a private girls' school.

Daniel needed little encouragement to join Martha at Annandale, while maintaining his office in the old schoolroom in next door Haberfield House. But the vast majority of his work was now required to be done at the Institute building in town and there were evenings when he did not get home until well after dark, when he would swallow a couple of glasses of wine and a sandwich, then virtually pass out in the marital bed until summoned at six the next morning by a knock on the bedroom door from 'good old Sarah', the former nurse turned housekeeper, who was now approaching her sixtieth year.

Relief of a sort was afforded to Daniel one day in early 1810, two months after the new governor, Lachlan Macquarie, had been installed. The days of the New South Wales Corps were numbered, since the new governor, an Army man, had come out at the head of his own regiment, the 73rd Regiment of Foot, giving the former Corps members the choice of re-enlisting or going into civilian life. It was one of them —

George's former Captain, Thomas Laycock — who was sheepishly admitted into Daniel's office on the first floor of the old Commissariat, looking for work.

'I was the one who found Governor Bligh under the bed,' Laycock reminded Daniel, 'and despite what he may insist, he was definitely looking for somewhere to hide.'

'You did your Major and the colony a great service that day,' Daniel conceded, 'but how do you think you may be of service to me?'

'Before I enlisted,' Laycock replied, 'I was the General Manager of a hardware store in Norwich and I know all about invoices, bills of account, stock-taking, bank documentation and the like.'

'With skills like that, why did you need to join the marines?' Daniel asked suspiciously.

Laycock flushed slightly as he replied, 'There was a girl … she broke my heart when she married someone else. But I'm over that now, since I met this lovely girl over here. She's not a convict, but her mother was and we got married only two months ago and now she wants me to give up the army and get a real job, but…'

Daniel raised a hand to silence him. 'I can relate to *all* of that. You start next Monday, at 7 a.m.'

Laycock proved to be so efficient that Daniel was able to spend more time on paperwork back at Haberfield, where Martha could join him on 'special' nights in their old bedroom, but events were not transpiring so happily in London, where George and John were incurring increasing expenditure as they awaited a date for the court-martial.

Ex-Governor Bligh had managed to persuade the Army Office, in a series of heated despatches from the other side of the world, that he would be required to give evidence if the entire process was not to be seen as a 'whitewash' and it was October of 1810 before he made it to London. By then he had been left in no doubt that his competence in running the colony would be the key factor in what was to follow and he wasted further time by insisting on being allowed to acquire affidavits from 'worthies' back in New South Wales regarding the true state of affairs when he had been deposed and the lack of justification for George's actions. He also sought to blame any unrest in the colony at the time on the undermining tactics of John Macarthur, who he demanded should be placed on trial for treason.

Elizabeth Macarthur was too proud to admit that John had recently lost money heavily on certain ill-advised side ventures and that it looked increasingly as if their entire empire would collapse in a pile of unpaid debts, and that John would end his days in a debtors' gaol in the land of his birth. She was forever plaguing Daniel with demands for advances of John's share of the partnership profits, even though the fleece count seemed to be diminishing at an alarming rate through the incompetence and basic dishonesty of a succession of farm managers whom she had employed without sufficient enquiry into their previous activities.

When Esther learned that Elizabeth was in effect making forward withdrawals on future profits, she demanded to know why and insisted that similar amounts should be credited to George's account in London, to defray his mounting expenses over there. Daniel was often on the point of either tearing out his own hair in sheer frustration and worry, or walking out of the partnership that was his only means of survival.

The court-martial, when it was finally convened, turned out to be the judicial equivalent of a draw. The judges were clearly not impressed by the grossly exaggerated claims of Bligh that

George and Macarthur had conspired to ruin the colony economically, to the point at which George could justify taking over as dictator, but neither did they accept that George had been left with no alternative once the governor began using the force of the law for his own personal ends. Their private opinion, exchanged during meal breaks, was that New South Wales was well rid of all three of them, but the final — official — ruling was that George was to be cashiered out of a regiment that no longer existed, but allowed to return to the colony as a civilian. Since this was all that he wanted to do anyway, he was more than satisfied with the outcome, but was deeply distressed when informed that Macarthur was to face trial for treason if he ever set foot back in the colony.

Back in the colony itself, their only knowledge of what was transpiring at the other end of the globe came via the despatches and other communications unloaded regularly from the *Parramatta* and by early in 1814 everyone was at their wits' end. Esther seemed to have aged twenty years since George's departure, and Martha's hair was now more white than black, despite her frequent resort to the latest product imported from London designed to reverse, or delay, the process. George Junior was threatening to throw in the towel if any more of the cattle out at the cow pasture were speared by natives, while Elizabeth Macarthur was searching desperately for another manager at Camden who was interested in sheep rather than either the money that could be siphoned off unlawfully, or her presence in his bed.

It was therefore a welcome break from all the trials and tribulations of holding it all together when Daniel found himself in the back office at Haberfield with Martha. The *Parramatta* had landed again that morning and he had been able to leave the supervision of its first unload in the capable, and now experienced, hands of Tom Laycock.

Suddenly they became aware of a coach careering up the front drive and its door being opened to the sound of a woman screaming. They hastily rose and rushed through to the front of the house, where Mary had opened the door and almost been flattened by a hysterical Roseanna as she rushed in.

'Come quickly — now! Oh *please*, help me! You've *got* to help me, please!'

Martha rushed forward, grasped Roseanna by the shoulders and shook her sharply. 'What is it? What's happened?'

'It's Mother — she's lying in the sitting room — I think she's dead!'

The one-mile coach ride between the properties seemed like ten miles and Daniel was out of the carriage and through the front door of Annandale House before it had even come to a halt. The children were gathered in a forlorn-looking cluster near the open door to the sitting room and Daniel brushed past them and ran in. Esther was lying slumped in an easy chair, head back, legs straight out in front of her, a peaceful smile on her face.

Martha rushed in behind him. 'Is she dead?'

'Dead drunk. It looks as if she knocked back an entire bottle of gin.'

'Why?'

'No idea — but this might give us a clue.'

There was a letter lying in the folds of Esther's skirts and Daniel picked it up and scanned it quickly, then gave a loud yell of joy. 'It's George — he's coming home on the next vessel! He's a free man and a civilian!'

25

'I can't believe this is all happening,' Daniel said for the tenth time that day, as he selected another glass of the champagne being brought round on trays by Sarah and Lucy, whose bulging apron confirmed that her marriage to Edward Tolhurst was proving fruitful.

'So you keep saying,' Martha replied as she shook her head at the proffered tray, 'but it's happening nevertheless, and the least you can do is to look happy for them.'

Two months earlier, George had been rowed ashore from the *Parramatta* to a large welcoming party of Johnstons and Bradburys, led by Esther, whose shrieks of joy as she threw herself at him could be heard all over the harbour. An hour later, as the coaches had delivered them all to the front door at Annandale, where the servants of both households had lined up outside to welcome the master home, George had stood surveying his front gardens for the first time in five years and thanking Daniel profusely for all his hard work in keeping things together in his absence.

'The thanks are all mine,' Daniel said as he followed George's gaze. 'Without your generous offer all those years ago, I'd now be facing the same dilemma as all the other men in the Corps — whether to go or stay. I've employed Tom Laycock at the Institute, by the way — I hope you don't mind, but he was a general store manager before he became a marine.'

'You must be a mind-reader,' George replied. 'He's going to be very useful for what I've been planning while gazing forlornly at the never-ending ocean. There'll have to be a few changes around the place, while John's still stuck in London.'

'Care to enlighten me, if it's going to involve me in more work?' Daniel asked.

'All in good time, Daniel. There's something very important I need you for first.'

The formal written invitations to the wedding of George and Esther fell like artillery shells onto the doorsteps of those who were invited. The shock had been less for Daniel and Martha, since they had been informed weeks beforehand that despite their many years and seven children, together — eight, if you counted Roseanna — George and Esther had never been married.

They had only found out then because Esther wanted Martha for her matron of honour, while Daniel was George's obvious best man. The Reverend Walker, newly arrived in the colony and anxious to become better known among his new flock, had sought the special licence of a totally indifferent governor to solemnise the proceedings in the drawing room at Annandale House.

After the ceremony, they had all transferred to the sitting room, where Daniel and Martha were now mingling with the other very select invitees. The governor, predictably, had declined on the ground of pressure of work brought on by the need to restore the colony after years of misrule, while other leading citizens had politely invented other excuses in their embarrassment at learning that for the best part of twenty years they had welcomed into their lives and homes a couple with seven children between them who had been living in sin.

Sadly, the most insulting refusal to attend had come from Elizabeth Macarthur, whose husband John had travelled to London in order to support George at his court-martial and who was now seemingly destined to remain there, afraid to return and face a treason trial. Not only had Elizabeth regarded it as gross disloyalty on George's part to return without him, but she had insisted on terminating the partnership with George and Daniel in order to claim John's portion of the capital due to him on the dissolution, which he urgently required for his continued sojourn in London.

From the bitter aftermath of what amounted to the closure of the Institute had, however, come some encouraging initiatives for the ongoing prosperity of those left to clean up the commercial wreckage. After several long evenings in intense debate over many wine decanters, George and Daniel had formed a new partnership. The lease on the Institute had been transferred, without any opposition from their notional landlord the governor, to an organisation calling itself the 'Colonial Theatre', which consisted of Martha and Esther with ongoing dramatic ambitions and their first production was well into the planning stage.

After it had been agreed that the back room in Haberfield House was more than adequate as a head office for the partnership, they had all sat down and debated how to arrange for the retail distribution of the goods returning on the *Parramatta* after its regular deliveries of Johnston beef to London. It had been Martha who had pointed out the absence in the town of any general store in which colonists could acquire hardware items such as household implements, shovels, ropes, cutlery and hand tools. The mention of 'hardware' had triggered a new line of thought in Daniel's mind and Tom Laycock had been delighted to be invited to resume his old trade as the manager of the proud new store in what had been the original wooden Governor's House on the quayside, which now proudly advertised above its entrance that it belonged to 'Johnston and Bradbury.'

'I *wasn't* being gloomy,' Daniel protested. 'Quite the opposite, in fact. I was just reflecting on how much life has changed for us all in twenty-six years. I was watching you standing next to Esther and remembering the first time you were lined up alongside each other, waiting to leave the *Lady Penrhyn*.'

'Don't remind me,' Martha replied with a shudder. 'I must have smelt like a chicken run after a rainstorm. But while it's been all rosy for us since then, do you think we've really succeeded in establishing anything worthwhile out here?'

'Funny you should ask that,' Daniel said. 'Let's go outside for a moment — I want to show you something.'

'I've seen it all afore, guv'nor,' Martha joked in her Cockney harlot voice. 'Them's all the same really — when yer've seen one, yer've seen 'em all, 'cept some's bigger than uvvers.'

'I'm serious,' Daniel insisted, as he led Martha by the hand through the French windows that had lately been installed to allow access to the rear garden that sloped down towards the harbour with an unbroken view of the distant township.

Daniel pointed with his outstretched arm at the just visible former Institute building. 'Take a look at your new theatre — the old Institute warehouse. Then look slightly to the right, where you can see the start of the Rocks area. That places the Colonial Theatre on a site just to the left of the Rocks, correct?'

'Correct,' Martha confirmed as she squinted into the distance.

'Can you remember something else that was located precisely there, before the old Commissary Store was constructed?'

'No — what?' she replied, genuinely puzzled.

'Well, it was the site of a large cooking tent that was the work station of the first forty women to be disembarked from the *Lady Penrhyn*. Your new theatre is standing exactly where you once baked loaves for the prisoners.'

Martha broke into a smile. 'Where Mary Murphy first offered you her dumplings!'

'Twenty-six years ago, what is now a rapidly growing township was a shingly beach dotted around with tents, on which people condemned to lengthy terms of imprisonment were set to work under the raw elements, using unfamiliar tools and exposed to hostile natives, snakes, mosquitos and storms. Now we have a settled community with shops, churches — even public houses. We have another one out at Parramatta and growing communities all along the Hawkesbury. All those original convicts are now free men and women with families and futures.'

'"Oh brave new world, that has such people in it,"' Martha quipped.

'Pardon?'

'Elizabeth Macarthur's not the only one who can quote Shakespeare. And I take back what I said about you being in a gloomy mood. Calls for a celebration.'

'We're in the middle of one, surely?' Daniel asked.

Martha leaned across and kissed him on the cheek. 'I was referring to the celebration that Mary Murphy has planned for you when she gets you home.'

A NOTE TO THE READER

Dear Reader,

By the middle years of the eighteenth century, the English gaols were bulging at the seams, grossly overcrowded to an inhumane degree that not even the brutal regime of those times could tolerate. There was a need to relieve the pressure and some genius in Whitehall lit upon the idea of warehousing, far away somewhere, the worst of those who had just escaped the death penalty by having it 'commuted' to a lengthy prison term. The first option — America — ceased to be available after 1776, but fortunately Captain James Cook had by then discharged his commission to discover the fabled southern land of *Terra Australis*, a mere eight months away by sea.

On 13th May 1787, the 'First Fleet' of eleven ships set sail from Portsmouth and most of those on board survived rough seas, cholera and starvation rations to make landfall at 'Sydney Cove' in late January of the following year. They were a contrasting mixture of convicts (743 men, women and children, some of them born during the crossing) and those who had guarded them during the voyage — marines, some with their wives in tow, but many of them single men drafted into uniform by adversities of their own. It was a one-way trip for them all and they stepped ashore from one living hell to another.

They had been uprooted from the lives with which they were familiar and transported into an alien world on the other side of the globe. They were decanted onto a shingle beach in blistering heat, scowled at by unwelcoming natives who had been there ahead of them for thousands of years and who knew how to survive in this unforgiving terrain. The newcomers were under orders to establish a new colony under the English crown, armed only with hand tools and an instinct to remain alive.

Their first crops failed, their few animals fell victim to native spears and there was insufficient fresh water. Even those who were not manacled in work parties constructing the first few huts that might protect them from the occasional wild storm, the incessant insects and the venomous snakes, could hardly feel other than rejected, unwanted by the softer society they had left behind, most of them for good.

The result was that they somehow clung to each other in their mutual misery, companions in exile and dependent upon each other for their very survival. Those who knew only how to live outside society continued to do so, while those who found comfort in the company of fellow human beings and sought solace in companionship, set about finding it. Apart from the inevitable convict liaisons there were also other hands reaching out across the class divide, forming relationships that back in 'the mother country' would have been unthinkable.

Modern Australia is the heir to many of these liaisons, the ultimate beneficiary of those first few boatloads who scrambled up the shingle of Port Arthur. We will never know precisely how they survived and prospered, but this first novel in the series is my conjecture as to what it must have been like.

Many of the characters encountered in the chapters you have just read actually led more or less the lives described. Major George Johnston and his common-law wife Esther Julian, who met on board the *Lady Penrhyn*, the various governors with their brief grip on power, John Macarthur and his wife Elizabeth — even James Ruse, the pioneer agriculturalist whose name is preserved in a contemporary highway west of modern-day Parramatta.

Only Daniel and Martha are fictitious, but I like to think that their experience was by no means unique. Unlikely liaisons were formed in the cauldron of those early colonial years and many of the Australian families of today can proudly trace their ancestry back to the 'battlers' who formed the first community of New South Wales. The subsequent fortunes of the Bradbury dynasty are charted in the novels that follow in this series and hopefully I have tweaked your interest sufficiently for you to wish to learn what happens to Daniel and Martha's firstborn, Matthew, in the next volume in the series, *Eye For An Eye*.

I'd love to receive feedback on this first novel, whether in the form of a review on **Amazon** or **Goodreads**. Or, of course, you can try the more personal approach on my website and my Facebook page: **DavidFieldAuthor**.

Happy reading!

David

davidfieldauthor.com

Sapere Books is an exciting new publisher of brilliant fiction and popular history.

To find out more about our latest releases and our monthly bargain books visit our website:
saperebooks.com

Made in the USA
Las Vegas, NV
04 April 2022

46838060R20133